WHISPERED LOVE

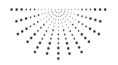

KATHLEEN BALL

This book is dedicated to all the friends I've made along the way. To Bruce, Steven, Colt and Clara because I love them.

CHAPTER ONE

"*P*lease, Da, please wake up," Patricia Clarke cried as she shook her father's shoulder. It was no use. His cold, stiff body told her he'd likely been dead since shortly after he'd gone to bed and now the break of dawn threatened. A strong wind blew through their canvas tent-like structure. Even the woody scent of fir needles didn't bring her the usual comfort. The rest of the company would be up in no time, and once they knew her father was dead, she'd be asked to leave.

She quickly gave him one last kiss on his cold cheek and set about getting dressed. First, she made sure her breasts were bound, and then she pulled on a grubby shirt and torn pants. A cap on her head, drawn low over her forehead came next. Finally, she took out a jar of ashes she kept under her bed and rubbed some on her face. And with that, the trans-formation from Patricia to Patrick was complete.

The lumberjacks thought her to be a weak boy, who was too wet behind the ears to pay too much attention to. Her father had been the cook. The best damn cook there ever was, and she helped him without pay. The outfit had figured it was enough that they allowed the cook's "son" to stay.

A bubble of panic rose. Now what? She'd be asked to leave, probably today. It was fall already in the Pacific Northwest. The weather was always a gamble this time of year. If it snowed too early she'd never make it to town in time.

Turning to her father, she reached down and pulled the blanket over his face. She'd have to make herself useful and maybe, just maybe they'd keep her on. Her hope dimmed as she thought about Samuel Pearce, the foreman. For some reason he didn't seem to be too fond of her.

Running out of the tent toward the cookhouse, she almost tripped on a tree root. She quickly regained her balance and found Samuel staring at her. It figured. She'd wanted the coffee on before he got up. She slowed her pace until she stood in front of him. He was such a tall man she had to crane her neck to see his face.

"Something on your mind, kid?"

His deep strong voice unnerved her. "My, my Da, he's dead." Her heart dropped at Samuel's silence. "I can make the coffee and feed all the men."

"You think so?" Samuel cocked his dark brow.

She puffed out her bound chest. "I know so, sir."

"Not today, kid."

"But—"

Samuel sighed and put his strong hand on her shoulder. "You just lost your father. Tomorrow will be soon enough for you to start. Besides, one day with Callins cooking and they'll be demanding to have you cook. If anyone gives you a hard time let me know. I'll get a couple of the men to build a coffin. We'll bury him in a few hours."

Patricia blinked back tears that threatened. Samuel being nice was something she had never expected.

THREE HOURS LATER, she stood at the grave, dry eyed. She'd have time enough later to cry. It took everything she had to keep her emotions in, but somehow she managed. Her heart lay shattered at her feet but boys didn't cry. She didn't look her age of eighteen. Her da often lamented that she should have been married with wee ones already, but it wasn't safe being a female in an all-men camp.

It would be harder to keep up her charade without her father, but somehow she'd have to do it. She'd seen what happened to women who were willing to come into the camps and she wanted no part of these men. They were harsh, ill-mannered timber beasts. Not all, but most. But it wasn't as though they were near any type of civilization.

It killed her to look so dirty all the time, but no one wanted to come too near a boy who never bathed or washed his clothes. Even these lumberjacks had their standards. That was why she loved the scent of pine so much. It smelled fresh and clean.

She had so much to figure out. What about the cabin her da had been building? She'd never be able to finish it herself. She'd have to pay someone to do it, and at a big price, she suspected.

One by one, the men left the grave until all that was left was her, a shovel, and a mound of dirt. He was her father, and it was her responsibility. Heaving a sigh of resignation, she grabbed the shovel and poured one pile of dirt after another onto her da's casket. He'd come to love living out here in the midst of tall trees and clear rivers. Things hadn't always been easy, but she'd had the feeling he meant to stay put this time. Just not in this way. Her heart grew heavier with each shovelful she tossed into the grave until he was buried. She'd make a wooden cross and carve his name into it as soon as possible.

The giant pines swayed back and forth as though saying goodbye and she swallowed hard against her grief. Carrying the shovel, she trudged to the tool shed. She opened the door and jumped when she saw Samuel inside.

Ducking her head she quickly put the shovel away and as she was about to leave he grabbed her arm.

He knows!

Samuel stopped her and looked at her hands. He shook his head. "Don't you know enough to wear gloves? Look at all those blisters. You'd best wash them. I know you have an aversion to water but clean them good. There's salve in the supply cabin. I'll get it and leave it on your bunk."

She stared at the ground and shuffled her feet back and forth.

"Why is it you almost never look at me when I'm talking to you? Look I know you're a good kid and all, but you need to toughen up if you plan to make it out here. You father was too soft on you. Clean up, use the salve, and get some rest. Tomorrow you do the cooking. Let me warn you. The men will give you a hard time. That's just the way it goes. You keep your head down and cook. Understand?"

She glanced up at him and nodded. "I understand."

"Good. You know it wouldn't kill you to clean the rest of you too."

Without a word she hurried from the shed. What she wouldn't give to be clean. Totally clean. She bathed often but afterwards she had to put ash on her face, a bit of dirt in her hair and wear the same old smelly clothes. It was her only protection against the men discovering her secret.

SAMUEL SAT at the small table in his cabin. As foreman, he had the biggest cabin. He didn't spend too much time in it.

Usually he sat in the cookhouse with a cup of coffee and did his paperwork. Not tonight. Everyone had liked and respected Walt Clarke, and his death had hit some hard. A few of the men were all for throwing Pat out of camp. They thought making him leave would finally make a man of him.

He'd been concerned enough someone would make the attempt that he had a couple of men standing guard at the boy's tent. Things would cool off by the morning. He just hoped Pat could cook. Foreman or not, there was nothing Samuel could do; if the boy couldn't do a man's work he was out.

THE NEXT MORNING, Samuel washed and got dressed. He tried to set a good example to the men. Not that it worked. Most only had one change of clothes and cleanliness wasn't too high on their list of priorities. They were a rough lot and there didn't seem to be a way to change them. They were hard workers though.

The ground was hidden by the fog and it always gave him an eerie feeling. Shrugging it off, he walked to the cookhouse, hoping all was going well. The guards were gone from the Clarke tent. Hopefully that was a good sign.

The smell of strong coffee filled the air, and he smiled. He nodded to the many greetings as he entered and sat at his table. His three right-hand men were already seated and eating. Leon Getty, Fred Bean, and Hank Blue were all good, loyal men. He trusted them implicitly, and the men knew to follow their orders. "How's the food?"

Leon wiped his mouth with his sleeve. "Better than old Walt. That boy has been working like crazy doing by himself but the biscuits are light, the hot cakes are good, and the eggs aren't brown."

Before he could say a word, Pat put a cup of coffee and a

plate of chow in front of him and hurried away. Pat still stank, but his hands were clean at least. Samuel eyed his food with interest. He picked up a biscuit, and it didn't feel like a rock. Next, he tried a bite of the hot cake. It too was light. And when he put a forkful of scrambled eggs in his mouth, he actually closed his eyes at the heavenly taste.

"Try the coffee, boss," Fred Bean encouraged.

He took a swig, and a jolt of surprise widened his eyes. That small boy knew how to cook a damn sight better than his old man had. Samuel realized that all chatter had ceased and everyone was watching him. He glanced in Pat's direction and read the worry on his face. "You done good, kid. Real good. You got yourself a job."

Pat's smile was bigger than Samuel had ever seen before. His shoulders relaxed and Samuel realized just how much Pat had riding on this one meal. He'd sure pulled it off.

Hank Blue slapped his hand down on the wooden table. "Looks like we have ourselves a cook!"

Noise once again took over the hall. And relief filled Samuel. He hated giving workers the boot. He never fired anyone without just cause, but he couldn't keep someone on just because his pa died either. He'd toughen up Pat in no time. The boy needed to be able to defend himself up here. Some of the men weren't the most savory characters, but they pulled their weight.

"Eat up. We have a lot to do before winter sets in. Leon make sure everyone has a place to winter. I don't want to bury any frozen loggers this year."

"Sure thing, boss. I might have to find someone willing to bunk with the boy. His pa never finished the cabin. I'll figure something out," Leon said as he stood to leave. "Sad thing about Walt." Fred and Hank both stood and followed Leon outside. Soon after the rest of the men followed and quiet fell over the cookhouse.

SAMUEL WATCHED Pat scramble to gather up all the dirty dishes and pile them on the counter near the stove. The piles were almost as tall as he was. He sure was a puny fella. "Got any family hereabouts?"

Pat turned. "No, it was just me and my da."

"Where are you from?"

"Ireland, County Tyrone. My mum died on the crossing. Da and I have traveled ever since. He was a wanderer, and he never planted his feet. This was the one place he wanted to stay." He sighed loudly. "He got his wish."

"As long as you pull your weight, you have a job here."

"Thank you." Pat turned back and started washing the dishes.

He was a strange little guy. But he could cook and that was all that mattered. Samuel stood and headed for the door.

PAT CLOSED her eyes and thanked God when Samuel left. She'd gotten the job. A huge weight lifted off her shoulders. Every bone in her body ached, and her blistered hands hurt, but in light of everything else none of that mattered. Now all she had to do was pay someone to finish the cabin and she'd be set for winter. She refused to think past winter. Right now, it was survival one day at a time. She was strong and tough where it mattered most—on the inside. She was a survivor.

She finished the last of the dishes but there was no rest to be had. Lunch needed to be started, and they'd be expecting a lot of food. Lunch usually included the great trinity of beans, pork, and bread. The loggers worked hard, and they needed to eat a lot more than the average man. It was hard physical labor the sawdust savages did, and they expected three good meals a day.

She'd put the pork and beans on, set the bread to rising, and then she'd check on the cabin and see what still needed to be done. This was the time she liked best, when all the men were working. She'd have to be quick about it. She had plenty of cooking to do. She hoped she'd be able to keep up with it all with her father gone.

Stepping outside, she noticed that the fog had lifted. Sometimes it lingered until afternoon but today it was clearing and a watery sun was trying to poke through the clouds. She walked past Samuel Pearse's cabin and not too far beyond that was the cabin her father had started. A bittersweet sensation filled her as she approached. The cabin would provide her with the shelter she needed, but her da wouldn't be there to share it with her. The structure was a one-room log cabin with a loft for her to sleep in. It had a wood stove but no roof. Three of the walls were completed with the fourth halfway up. It seemed like there was still a lot to do, but somehow she'd get it completed.

Sorrow encased her and refused to let go. It was the way of things, she supposed. She turned and walked out of what would be the doorway when Big Hans stepped into her path. She had no liking for the big blond brute. A shiver of fear went up her spine.

"You'll be needing a protector up here now. I'd be happy to do it for a price." He smiled a sickly almost toothless smile. His beard had food in it, and his breath was fetid. He wasn't a man to tangle with. He'd even tried to buy her from her da.

"I work this camp just like any other man. I'm under the protection of the lumber company and Samuel Pearse. You know better."

"Your pappy ain't here no more, so I say you're fair game.

I have an itch that only you can take care of, and I aim to have ya." His voice was low and filled with malice.

Pat backed up until she hit the partially built wall. "I'll scream."

"Just like a little sissy boy. I'd enjoy hearin' ya scream."

She quickly dodged his hands, clambered over the half wall, and climbed the ladder to the loft. Then she used all her strength to drag the ladder up with her. Her arms felt as though they'd been pulled out of their sockets.

His face was mottled red. "Get down here," he roared. "You'll be sorry when I get my hands on you."

"I'm not going to let you touch me. Find someone else!"

"Why should I? I've got you, and I will have you one way or the other. Now get down here."

Leon Getty suddenly appeared. "Hans you're docked a day's pay. Any more threats and you're out of here."

"We'll see about that. I'm the strongest one you've got. I'll get back to work." He turned and glared at her causing her to shiver.

"Pat, I need you. Samuel's been hurt. Just shove the ladder off the edge and I'll put it up so you can get down."

"Thanks, Leon." She gave the ladder a shove and cringed at the pain in her shoulders. She watched Leon put the ladder up and hold it as she climbed down. "How hurt?"

"Hurt enough to need a bit of doctoring. Come on." Leon raced out the doorway.

She had to run to keep up with Leon's long stride. Thank goodness, it wasn't far to Samuel's cabin. She braced herself not knowing what to expect. Sometimes men came back with missing limbs. She should have participated more when her father doctored the men. She knew a lot but watching wasn't the same as doing.

The door to the cabin was open, and she breathed a sigh of relief when she saw Samuel sitting on a chair holding his arm. No blood poured off him. That was a good start. She hurried over to him.

"What happened?" she asked.

"My arm got caught between a tree and the dirt," he gritted out.

"It could be crushed. Take off your shirt and I'll have a look." Her mouth went dry as Leon helped him out of his shirt. The muscles on his chest were chiseled and covered in a sprinkling of dark hair. His stomach was flat and tight and his shoulders... Oh my, his shoulders. She shook her head. It was his arm that was injured, not the rest of him.

Pulling a chair next to him, she sat down and gingerly examined his arm. He winced only once. He had a dark bruise already spreading over most of his upper arm and a long jagged gash oozing blood.

"It's badly sprained and in need of stitches. It'll heal nicely as long as you don't use it. I mean it—you'll have to keep it still. You're lucky you didn't crush your arm."

"As soon as it happened I was sure that would be the outcome. Thanks, kid. I can still work, though."

Men were so stubborn. "No. You can tell people to work, but you're not to lift a thing. I'm going to splint your arm, and you'll need to keep it in a sling."

He frowned. "For how long?"

"Four weeks at least. Leon, can you get me bandages?"

"Sure thing." He hurried out of the cabin.

Samuel sniffed the air. "You stink, you know. You're going to have to take a bath if you're to help me." He held her gaze.

"Help you do what? I already have a job."

"For starters, you can help me dress and do a few things as they come up." His brow furrowed. "Maybe you should move your cot in here."

"With you?" She shook her head and took a step back.

"What about Leon? Or there is always Fred and Hank. Their job is to help you."

"I suppose you're right, but I still want you in clean clothes come morning. You hear me?"

Pat looked away and nodded. Life was just about to get even harder.

CHAPTER TWO

Up before the sun, Pat quickly dressed in clean clothes. She'd taken great pains to bind her troublesome breasts extra tight. She'd even cut her hair shorter late last night. No one except for Big Hans ever bothered with her, so maybe, just maybe, she'd pull it off. Sometimes people saw what they expected to see, and they all expected her to be a boy.

She pulled on her boots and left her tent, surprised to see a lamp lit in Samuel's cabin. Part of her wanted to knock on the door and see if he was feeling all right, but a bigger part of her warned her away. Trouble came her way often enough; she didn't need to go looking for it.

She strode into the cookhouse, lit the big cook stove, put the coffee on, and started to mix the dough for the biscuits. A slight chill lingered in the air; it was fall all right. She rolled out the dough and began to cut rounds for the biscuits, so deep in thought she didn't notice the door opening. She did hear it close. Startled, she looked up, braced to run in case it was Hans.

Instead, it was Samuel appearing weary and in pain. His

face was unshaven which was very unusual for him. He looked very appealing, and her thoughts disturbed her. Men were the enemy, and they were to be avoided at all costs.

"Are you alright?" she asked as she wiped the flour off her hands and made her way toward him.

"I'm fine. I just didn't get to sleep much, and it was a bit difficult getting my shirt on."

She glanced at his chest. He had his shirt on but it wasn't buttoned. "I thought one of your men was staying with you." She reached out and immediately began to button up his shirt.

"Leon stayed last night. He snores too loud, and he's near impossible to wake up. I'm not sure how much help he'll end up being. I think I'll try Fred Bean tonight." He stared at her. "You look good all clean kid. Too bad there aren't any females around. You'd strike their fancy I think."

Pat blushed. "I ain't looking for any troublesome female."

"Maybe he don't like women," Big Hans said as he barged into the hall.

"Big Hans, we don't insult the cook," Samuel said his voice held a warning.

"I invited Pat here to live with me through the winter."

Her breath stalled in her chest as her heartbeat quickened. "I declined."

"It's going to be a long cold winter." Hans licked his lips.

"Like I said, Hans, don't insult the cook. Pat, can you fix this sling for me before you get back to work?" Samuel walked over to his dining table and sat down. Then he turned and stared Big Hans down until he left. "Sorry about him."

Pat sat down next to Samuel and rolled up his sleeve. She'd never noticed how nice he smelled before. The scent of pine and wood and soap clung to him. It was a nice combination. She checked his wrappings to be sure they were still tied securely to the wood splints. Satisfied they were tight, she rolled his sleeve back down and retied his sling. Being near him was discomforting, and she couldn't figure out why.

"You look much better cleaned up, Pat. I think you'll find being clean isn't a hard thing to accomplish."

She quickly nodded and started to stand but stopped when she noticed several small cuts along his jaw. She reached out and touched the side of his face. "What happened?"

He smiled and shrugged. "I tried to shave this morning."

"With one hand? Not very wise. I could…"

"Could what?"

She quickly got up and went back to her biscuit cutting. "I helped my da shave is all. I was going to offer to help but a beard is a fine thing to have." She touched her own chin. "I can't wait to be able to grow one."

Samuel laughed. "I think it'll be a year or two before that happens, Pat. Don't worry about it. I might just take you up on your offer though. I like being clean-shaven. How about some coffee? Is it ready?"

Her heart beat faster at the thought of standing near him to shave him. Oh, Lord. What had she been thinking to make such an offer? "Um, yes. I'll bring you a cup." She poured the coffee and brought it over to him. His intense stare scared her. It was though he could see right through her. "I'd best get a wiggle on and make breakfast."

"No hurry, I'm just happy with my coffee."

Giving him a quick nod, she hustled off. There was no way he could tell she was female. She'd work on making her voice deeper. If worse came to worst she could always put a scar on her chin or something. Nope, that would only bring attention to the fact she had no whiskers. Damn she missed her father.

The biscuits were baking, the ham was frying, and she was busy making batches of eggs. There wasn't much time to think. There'd been a few comments about her appearance. None were appreciated. She needed to practice making her eyes look beady too. There was no one to hide behind. She was on her own.

She grabbed the coffee pot and walked over to the fore-man's table, refilling Samuel's, Leon's, Fred's, and Hank's cups. It was something she'd done a hundred times before but this time her heart beat faster.

"Hey, kid, do you snore?" Leon asked.

"How would I know?" Darn her voice sounded too deep.

Fred laughed. "Yes Leon, how would he know?"

Leon frowned. "His pappy would have told him." He looked up and stared at her. "Well? Did your pappy ever mention you snoring?"

"Now that you mention it, he said I snored louder than anyone he knew. Kept him up at night, I did." She swallowed hard hoping they believed her. She wasn't about to get roped into staying at Samuel's house. "I have plenty of men to feed." She turned and walked away, feeling the heat of Samuel's stare on her.

Samuel groaned in pain. He hadn't taken anything for it, he figured he'd tough it out. It was right before supper and he couldn't take it anymore. He'd have to see if Pat knew anything more about healing. There was laudanum but he saved that for men who lost limbs. Not for a simple sprain. Pat's father had known a lot about herbs and hopefully he'd passed his knowledge on.

Gritting his teeth, he walked over to the cookhouse. The boy was hard at work. Losing his father pushed him to mature it seemed. Pat's head snapped up when Samuel entered.

"What happened?" Pat asked.

"I look that bad?"

"You're pretty white-faced." Pat wiped his hands on a towel and rounded the serving table. "Sit down before you fall down."

He grunted but did as Pat asked. "Do you have anything for pain?"

"Laudanum."

"No, I'm saving that in case the men get clumsy. Walt always had a stash of herbs."

Pat nodded and gave him a sad smile. "He loved harvesting and drying the plants. He was really good at that. Saved more than one life. Let me check and see if we have some skullcap. It should lessen the pain and take some of the swelling down."

"I'd appreciate it." He watched as Pat rummaged through the shelves. He'd take out a glass bottle, look at it and put it back. Finally, he seemed to find the one he looked for. He turned, holding up the bottle, and smiled.

"I'll just make a quick tea for you."

Samuel nodded and watched the boy. There was something different about him, and it wasn't only that he was clean. He couldn't figure it out. Not that it really mattered. The boy knew how to cook, and that was all that counted.

After a bit, Pat put a cup in front of him. Samuel nodded his thanks and then took a sip. It wasn't bad at all, and he'd expected bad. "Thanks, kid. Your father taught you well."

"He did at that. I know about as much as he did about healing and the like. But until now I just mostly watched."

Samuel nodded. "You're earning your wages. I like a man who pulls his weight." It surprised him to see Pat blush.

The door opened, and the men started pouring in. Pat

quickly went back behind the serving table and dished out supper. Samuel was disgusted by the leer Big Hans gave the kid. That man was a predator. He waited until his three right hand men sat down. "How'd everything go today?"

Leon began running down the events of the day.

Samuel listened with half an ear until Leon paused in his report. "Put Pat's gear in my cabin. I bet he doesn't really snore."

"Sure thing, boss," Hank said.

The one thing Samuel hated about Hank was he always talked with his mouth full of food. Many of the men did. Samuel sat across from Leon whenever possible to avoid seeing it.

Fred laughed. "I think Big Hans will be jealous."

Samuel nodded. "That's another reason I want Pat in my cabin. His tent won't keep Hans out. If he didn't do the work of three men, I'd have fired him long ago. I'm heading back to my cabin. I'm feeling the effects of the tea I had. It took away a lot of pain but I'm feeling tired."

"Don't you worry, boss. We'll have Pat all moved in tonight."

Samuel nodded and left. It was a cool, crisp night. Logging season would be at a snail's pace before he knew it. A lot of the men spent the harsher part of winter hunting and trapping. Pelts brought in a lot of money. They had to be careful though. Both the Indians and the French trappers didn't care to have their areas poached. Sometimes it was downright dangerous. So far, they hadn't caused any trouble for the logging company, but that could change with one incident.

"WHAT DO you mean I have to pack up my things? I already

tol' ya I snore louder than a choked bull." Pat crossed her arms and tried to give Leon her best glare.

"Boss's orders. I think he liked that tea you made. Doesn't much matter he said to move you and that's what I aim to do. Do you want your pappy's things or should I hand out what's usable?"

She gritted her teeth. Leon wasn't backing down. "I'll take it all. Not that he had much."

"Well, get to it. I don't have all night to babysit ya." Leon walked out of the tent and sat in front of the door.

There'd be no time for reminiscing and grieving. Her shoulders slumped as she grabbed a bag and filled it with her things. She did the same for her father's things. She hadn't come across a stash of money. It had to be there somewhere. Her da had always squirrelled away money in case he got the urge to move on again. It was their insurance against the rest of the world. Frantically, she searched under the cots and beneath the pot-bellied stove. She studied the ground for any sign of digging.

She found nothing.

Her heart sank, and she felt ill. Where was it? Her mother's brooch was with the money. The brooch didn't have much value, but it meant a lot to her. She sat on the ground and put her face in her hands. Now what? Someone in the camp was a thief. No one had dared to steal from her father, but they apparently had no problem stealing from her.

"You about done?" Leon asked as he walked into the tent. "What's wrong with you?"

Not knowing who she could trust, she shrugged her shoulders. "Nothing." She stood and swung a bag over each shoulder. "Let's go."

Dread filled her with each step she took. This was the worst idea possible. How was she going to keep Samuel from finding out her secret? This wasn't going to be easy.

Her face heated at the thought of sleeping in the same cabin as Samuel. How was she supposed to get her cabin finished without money? She was trapped good and tight this time. Once discovered, Samuel would throw her out.

Oh Da, why did you leave me?

Samuel nodded to her as she walked in. He sat at a table with two chairs. Looking around her stomach cramped. It was one big room. She'd hoped he slept in a separate room. For a second she forgot to breathe. "Nice place," she choked out. She set both bags on the floor, taking note of the big bed in one corner of the room and the cot not too far away from it. It boasted a cook stove that was bound to keep them warm all winter. All winter, if she lasted through fall.

"I hope you don't mind staying with me for a bit. This sprained arm is a nuisance, and I could use the help."

She tilted her head as she studied him. He seemed so sincere. It would be hard but she might just pull it off. She'd just go back to being dirty boy Pat. He'd keep his distance.

"Well, if that's all, I have a card game to get to," Leon said. "Let us know in the morning if he snores like a choked bull like he claims." Leon chuckled as he left.

"A choked bull?" The humor in Samuel's eyes annoyed her.

"Yes, that's what I've been told. Now, where can I move the cot to?"

"There's no need to move it. Both beds are out of the way."

She furrowed her brow. "I suppose so, but I've never liked sleeping too close to anyone."

Samuel laughed. "I know I smell just fine. If anything I'd think people would want to move away from you. Just leave them. You can stash your belongings under your cot, and you can hang your clothes on the pegs. I do expect you to bathe and wash your clothes. Did your father lose his sense of smell somewhere along the way?"

There he went with humor in his eyes again. "I'll do what I can, and no my father was just fine. He was a strong man and a good man." She lifted her chin a mite.

"You must take after your ma. Bet she was a good looking lady."

Pat hung up a shirt and some pants. "You know, you make me nervous with all your chatter. You wouldn't be like Big Hans or something would ya? I'll fight you the whole way. I don't go in for such things." She turned and gazed at him.

She wanted to laugh at his wide-eyed look of shock. Maybe that would keep him off her trail for a while. "Is there anything you need help with before shut-eye?"

"I'd appreciate it if you'd help me with my shirt and pants. And no, I'm not like Big Hans. I happen to like my women nice and curvy if you know what I mean."

Pat nodded. "That's how I like mine too."

Samuel threw his head back and laughed. "I wouldn't have thought you'd been with any women yet. But gentlemen don't kiss and tell, do they?" He unbuttoned his shirt as he crossed the room to his bed. "Help me get this off."

She wished she could close her eyes instead of having his massive chest in front of her. "Sure thing." She'd never been tempted by a man before, and she was having a hard time keeping her hands steady. She pushed his shirt off his shoulders and carefully took his injured arm out of the sleeve. "Do you want it hung on a peg?"

"Yes, both my pants and shirt if you don't mind." He was having difficulty unbuttoning his pants.

Closing her eyes, she did it for him and slid them down his legs. When she opened her eyes, she gulped. She wanted to touch him, all of him. Quickly she turned away, pants in hand, and then she hung them up. She scrambled to blow out the lamp and dove into her bed.

"You sleep in your clothes?" His deep voice made him seem closer to her than he really was.

"What's it to you?" she challenged.

"Nothing, good night." She heard him trying to get comfortable, and soon his breathing was nice and even. Now if only she snored like a choked bull she'd be out of the cabin and back into her tent by late morning.

SHE WOKE the next morning early as usual. It took her a moment to orient herself. Peeking over, she could make out the shape of Samuel in his bed. It wasn't a good sign. She must not snore. She didn't think she did, but she had hoped. The binding around her chest seemed tighter than usual. What she wouldn't give to be able to let her breasts free. Maybe when she went into the deep woods to relieve herself… She shook her head. No, it was too much of a gamble. Quietly, she got out of bed.

"Could you help me dress before you go?"

Dang it! "Sure, let me light the lamp." Cursing her luck, she lit the lamp and grabbed Samuel's clothes. He was sitting on his bed waiting for her. She quickly got his trousers on, and she was extra careful of his arm as she put his shirt on. She accidently touched his stomach with her fingers and he gasped. The air was practically crackling around them, but she pretended it wasn't happening.

"There, all done. I have to go I don't want the other men angry with me and all." She didn't wait for his reply. She practically stumbled in her haste to leave the cabin. Once outside she raced to the rear of the cabin. She rested her back against it for a moment, trying to catch her breath. Then she did what she usually did. She went deep into the woods.

Usually her father had stood guard, but now she just had to be smart about it.

Her necessary morning ritual complete, she marched to the cookhouse shaking her head. What she really needed was to find the darn, stinking thief that stole her money. She needed her own cabin before the first snow.

CHAPTER THREE

*I*t'd been two weeks since Pat moved in with him, and Samuel was fit to be tied. No amount of hints or good examples made a difference with that boy. He needed a bath, plain and simple. One bath a year just wasn't cutting it. He had clean clothes hanging on a peg, but he wore the same filthy garments every day.

Samuel shook his head. Tonight was bath night. Fred had come over and put water on to heat. They waited until they saw Pat leave the cookhouse, and then Fred filled the tub with the water and hurried away. He didn't want to be part of the fuss Pat was sure to make.

Samuel braced himself. He still couldn't use his arm but he hoped ordering the kid to clean up would be enough. There was no way he could wrangle him.

Pat entered the cabin, squinted his eyes at the tub, and shook his head. "If bathing is what you want you should have asked Leon or someone to help you. It's getting late, and I'm tuckered out." He made a beeline for his bed.

"It's not for me. It's for you."

"You have a good sense of humor, boss. I like to wash in the river. Thanks, but no thanks."

Samuel frowned. "You actually wash? When was this?"

Pat put his hands on his hips. "I wash every day."

"Good, you can wash here today. Now get to it. My cabin reeks, and I don't like it." He watched as Pat's eyes grew wide.

"I'll need some privacy," he said in a soft voice.

"I won't look. Just get on with it." Pat looked scared as all get out. He sighed and relented. "I'll be outside if you need me. Mind that you wash good, you hear?"

"Yes, I hear you," Pat grumbled. He had that mulish look on his face again.

Samuel grabbed his pipe and tobacco and took a seat outside the cabin. He filled the pipe and lit it, breathing in deep. Something bad must have happened to that boy. He was too skittish about anyone getting too close or looking at him. He must have fallen prey to someone like Big Hans. Poor kid. He'd heard initial splashing but now all was quiet.

He emptied out his pipe and knocked on the door. He waited but Pat didn't answer. Impatient and tired, Samuel walked into his cabin and stopped in his tracks.

Pat had fallen asleep in the water but the disturbing part was Pat's breasts showing above the water. What the hell? He couldn't help but stare. Pat was a she? He walked closer and yes, Pat was female all right, right down to her tiny toes. God, she was beautiful, and it was no wonder she didn't want to bathe with anyone around. Who knew her dirty streaked hair was actually a beautiful, bright blonde?

Grabbing the towel he called Pat's name again. This time she stirred and her eyes widened in panic.

He glanced away from her. "I'm not looking. Just take the towel, dry off, and get dressed. I think we need to talk."

She took the towel from him, and he turned his back to her. How the hell had this happened? Why would her father bring her to a logging camp of all places? Hadn't he realized the danger? He'd have to get her down off the mountain and quick before anyone found out. The men would turn her into a camp whore in a flash. Growing up, he'd seen it happen plenty of times.

He'd always had a firm rule of no women in his camp. He heard her getting dressed and all he could think of was her creamy, well-shaped breasts with dusky pink nipples. She was curvy, just the way he liked his women.

"I'm all dressed now, boss. Listen, I'm sorry for deceiving you but I didn't think I had a choice. You'd have thrown me away when my Da died if you had known. It wasn't my idea to live with you. I just wanted to do my job and be left alone. I planned to have the cabin my da started finished, but someone stole our money."

He turned and gazed at her. How he could have thought her a boy he didn't know. She was as pretty as they came. Her features were all fine. No wonder she wanted to look dirty. "Someone stole your money? When was this? Your father—"

"I noticed it when I packed up to move in here. Our money and my mum's broach were gone."

"How much did you lose? And don't lie. I know how much I paid your father."

Her mouth formed a thin line, and she crossed her arms across her chest. "I don't lie. Truthfully, I'm not sure how much was taken, but there was enough to finish the cabin. He ordered some supplies for the cabin, and they should be on the next supply wagon." Her shoulders slumped. "I'll leave in the morning. I know about the no-women rule you have. It's a good rule but..."

He couldn't take his gaze off her fine features and her pretty hair. "How do you hide your, um, your femaleness?"

Her brow furrowed, and when she turned red, he was relieved he didn't have to explain what he meant.

"I bind them with cloth."

"I see." He saw too much to ever pretend she wasn't bountiful. "You're shaking."

Pat clasped her hands together. "Everything has been so uncertain since Da died. It's taken everything within me to keep from being discovered. But now you know. I'll just take what you owe me, and I'll make my way down the mountain."

"Payroll is on the next supply wagon." He watched her wilt, but it was for her own good. It was too dangerous for her to meander down the mountain.

"I'll be gone in the morning. I'm not your problem. I was raised to be strong. You're a good man, Samuel. Another man would have had me flat on my back by now. You're a true gentleman. If I could just take some food with me—"

"You're not going anywhere." She winced at his gruff voice. "Here I can protect you. It's too dangerous this time of year. Fall can be long but most times winter comes before you know it, and I don't want to have to worry about you making it to town."

"I can go back with the supply wagon."

"The wagons stay here, and we turn them into sleds for the next run. I can't risk the lives of others. It's too unpredictable up here. I see the doubt in your eyes, but I'm talking from experience. We work as much as we can in the snow but there comes a point where you have to concede that the weather has won." He took a step forward and cupped her shoulder with his good hand. The feelings she evoked inside him almost knocked him down. He wasn't the type to mollycoddle or feel sorry for anyone, yet here he was doing both. "Listen, stay. Be the cook—as a boy—and we'll get through it. I promise."

Her green eyes stared into his, assessing him, taking his

measure and finally she nodded. "No more complaints about how dirty I am. I hate it just as much as you, but there's no help for it."

"I suspect we can find a way for you to look dirty without the stench. The men already think you stink, so I don't think they'll get too close. You've played your part well. Very well. So, we're in agreement, then? You'll stay?"

"Yes, I'll stay, but I think I should move back to my tent."

"No, you're staying here where I can protect you."

"But maybe I can get my cabin built."

"Maybe you can, but it won't be anytime soon. You need the supplies, and you'll need a few strong men to help you."

She stepped away from him and sank onto her bunk. "I suppose you're right. Thank you for not throwing me out. And for keeping my secret."

He nodded. "I need some shuteye." He pulled the tub across the floor and out the door where he emptied it. From the sounds of it, a hearty game of poker was going on in one of the other men's cabins, while the mournful music of a harmonica floated through the air. He had a bad feeling about this whole thing with Pat. Damn her father for bringing her here. He sighed. She was now his problem. Upon carrying the tub back inside, he saw Pat already in bed, pretending to be asleep. He hoped she wasn't afraid of him. She'd been around too many rough men lately.

MORNING CAME none too early for Pat. She'd tossed and turned all night and was glad to be out of bed. She quickly put on some clean clothes and pulled her cap over her hair.

"Light the lamp, Pat."

She did as he bid. "I want to get the coffee on and the biscuit dough ready. I'll be back for you."

"You can't go out looking like that."

"I'll rub some dirt on me after I take care of some private stuff." Her face heated.

"Just where do you go?"

"I go down past my cabin and there are some dense woods there. I've never run into anyone out there."

"I'll find a chamber pot or something for you. Make sure you use the clay to rub on. It stains your clothes so even when you're clean you'll look like you smell. Before you go, can you help me dress? I could ask someone else but they'd find that suspicious."

She nodded at his wisdom. Grabbing his shirt and pants, she knelt in front of him getting his legs in the pants. Pulling them up she stood and his heart-stopping chest was bare right in front of her. She tried to ignore the stirring in her stomach. She put his sprained arm through the sleeve first then the other arm. She practically gasped whenever her hand accidentally touched his skin. He left her mouth dry. "That should do it. Do you want to rest for a bit or do you want to come with me now?"

"I'll come with you." He groaned as he stood.

"Is your arm still hurting?"

"No, it's not my arm." He gave her a wicked grin and started for the door.

She shrugged, wondering what part of him was hurting. Then she quickly followed him as he made his way past her cabin.

"Which way?" he asked.

She pointed to the right. "I'll be right back." She was relieved when he nodded. For a moment, she thought he meant to go with her.

She finished painting herself with the clay and headed back to Samuel. She heard voices and wasn't sure what to do.

"There you are," Samuel said. "I was just telling Big Hans how you're looking for a plant to relieve the pain."

Hans leered at her, and she turned away from him. "Saw some but they need to mature a bit. I should be able to harvest then in about a week. I need to get that coffee made."

"Let's get going. See you in a bit, Hans," Samuel said in a firm voice.

"Later, boss." He cocked his eyebrow at Pat before he moved on.

"It'd be best if you stayed out of his way."

"I know he seems to like young boys. He looks at me like he can't wait to have me." She shuddered.

"I'll keep an eye on you best I can, but I won't always be where you are. Do you know how to fight?"

"I know enough to knee a man where it hurts and try to scratch his eyes out, but these men seem a bit big."

"I'll teach you to use a knife starting tonight."

"What about your sprained arm?"

"I only need one good arm to throw one."

They entered the cookhouse, and she gestured for him to sit in his chair. "No special treatment. Don't even look at me. I'm better off if I don't call attention to myself. And wrinkle your nose at me like you usually do."

"I wrinkle my nose at you?"

"You always do. I didn't mind. That's what the stench was for. You didn't want to get too close to me now, did ya?"

Samuel laughed a deep laugh. "So true. I'll treat you the same as before."

If only he'd kept his word. All through breakfast, he stared at her and it made her clumsy. She dropped a dozen eggs, and her biscuits weren't as light. She ended up with too many eyes upon her. As much as she tried to ignore him, her gaze fell upon him one time too many. This needed to stop.

She'd been playing the part of a boy for so long, she'd

forgotten about attraction between men and women. Of course, she'd thought about a family and children. She just never gave the husband much thought. Not that she'd met anyone halfway decent before. Before the lumber camp, her and her father had tried their luck mining for gold. Talk about a ruthless, cutthroat group of men.

She sighed. She'd been around these types of men so long, she probably didn't have the manners or social graces for a normal man. She stacked the dirty dishes and dug right in washing them. She had more important things on her mind than good manners. By the time she'd have the dishes done, it would be time to plan the next meal. It sure kept her busy.

"Hey, Pat, grab a cup of coffee and sit with me for a minute," Samuel called to her.

Her body stiffened. What part about not drawing attention to her didn't he understand? She poured herself some coffee and strode over to the table. "What can I do for you?"

"Can you hold this piece of paper in place while I tally up the numbers? It keeps moving."

She sat in a chair next to him and put her hand at the top of the paper, hoping it wouldn't take long. Bored, she read the paper and shook her head. "You added wrong."

"Nice try. Really I need to get this done."

"Nice try, what? You added wrong."

Samuel glanced up at her and gave her a hard stare. "What would you know about adding?"

She shook her head. "Nothing, never mind."

"Where did I go wrong?" he asked.

She smiled. He was taking her seriously. "See this column? She pointed to the second column on the page. You added the last number in twice."

He ran his finger down the column as he read. "Well I'll be darned. I didn't take you for a learned woman."

"Boy," she hissed. "Do not think of me as female at all. It'll only lead to slip ups."

Nodding he smiled. "You're better than me at this whole thing."

"You mean adding?"

"That too. I just need to sign this and I'll leave you be."

She watched as he corrected his mistake and signed the paper. Then she stood, took her coffee with her, and headed back to the pile of dishes.

CHAPTER FOUR

*S*amuel walked down the most used of the logging roads to the new section they were cutting. The air was crisp, and although much of the forest was made up of towering pine trees, there was enough other foliage to create a beautiful array of fall colors. Timber was where the money was now. He hadn't wanted any of the men to know, but he was the owner of the outfit, not just the foreman. As foreman, he was one of them. He got the respect. But as owner, he'd be the outsider. They'd never look at him as a lumberjack. He'd just be the guy who never paid them enough.

His outfit paid better than most, but there was always grumbling. There were always a few men who were rabble-rousers. It wasn't anything he couldn't handle. He liked being up on the mountain, away from the trappings of home. Especially Linda George. No matter how far away he moved, she always found him, declaring she couldn't live without him. Damn his family for putting such ideas in that simple minded, selfish girl.

No matter where he went, his parents paid her way so she could follow. He tried to buy her off but his offer didn't include enough money. He'd been tempted to shake her when she told him so. Now the mountain was his refuge. He'd hoped she'd go home. The town below didn't have anything fancy, including lodging. Last he heard, though, she was still down there waiting.

The sound of sawing and trees falling came from just ahead. They'd made good progress this year so far. There were enough trees and land for a lifetime of cutting. Up ahead he spotted Fred Bean with his notebook, keeping tally of how many trees and who cut them.

"Hey, boss, are you supposed to be up here?" Fred asked when Samuel was by his side.

"I'm fine. My arm will take a while to heal, and I can't do any more paperwork today. Everything looks great. You're doing a hell of a job out here."

Fred smiled. "It's the finest timber I've ever seen. How's it going with your roommate?"

Samuel shrugged. "He's a quiet kid. I got him to bathe, but he must roll in mud or something."

Fred laughed. "At least he doesn't snore."

"That is the bright side. How is the men's morale?"

"You know. This time of year, they're realizing they'll be stuck up here all winter. There's the usual griping about no women and liquor to pass the time with."

"There's plenty to do even in cold weather. Repairs on equipment and chopping wood come to mind too. We'd best get a few men on that full time so we have a decent amount to start with."

Leon Getty walked up with his bandana in his hand. He mopped up the sweat along his forehead. "I know it's getting cooler, but it's still hard work. Hey, boss. I heard you and the kid were out foraging in the woods this morning." Leon chuckled.

"His pa always had a stash of herbs for pain and healing,

and Pat wanted to replenish the supply. I didn't want him getting lost, so I tagged along."

"It wouldn't be Indian healing would it? I don't go in for that," Leon said.

"Nothing wrong with it, and it helps. Is Hans running his mouth about me?"

"You and everyone else," Leon said.

"I wish he'd gone back to town with the last supply wagon. He can be nasty." Fred commented.

"As long as he doesn't cross the line and does his work, he'll stay. No law saying we have to like all the workers." Samuel said smiling. He'd keep his own eye on Hans. No sense alerting others about the way Hans looked at Pat. Maybe Hans knew Pat was a woman. Either way he didn't want Hans and Pat alone ever.

Hank came running up the road. "Supply wagon is here, and there's a special delivery for ya, boss."

Samuel frowned. "Special?"

Hank put out his hand. "Yep, she's about this high with the prettiest red and yellow hair."

"Strawberry blond," Samuel automatically corrected.

"So, you do know her!" Hank nodded looking pleased.

"What the hell is Linda George doing here?"

Hank laughed. "Somethin' about stubborn men and what women have to go through, the usual woman complaint. My guess is she's hunting a husband and you're in her sites. Leastways you won't be lonely this winter."

"Fred, supplies for the Clarke cabin should be among the wagons. Get some men on getting that place done. Miss George will need a place to stay. Have her stow her stuff at my place for now. Pat and I can move into the unfinished cabin. For now we can at least stretch canvas over part of the roof. I'll be down in a bit."

Both Fred and Hank nodded and hurried down the path. Samuel took a deep breath and let it out slowly.

"I didn't know you were getting married," Leon commented as he wrote more numbers down.

"I'm not. According to my family and hers we're a perfect match, but there is no way I'm going to marry that one. A woman in camp will just be trouble. I trust these men as far as their skill with an ax goes, but around a woman? No."

"Supply wagon isn't going back," Leon stated, shaking his head.

"I think that was the whole plan. I'd better go make sure she doesn't start any trouble."

"I thought it was the men who would be the troublemakers?"

Samuel frowned. "Linda could give them a run for their money. There is no way she's going to like living up here." He nodded at Leon and turned to walk down the dirt road. Why would she be so reckless? Didn't he have enough going on with Pat? Damn! Pat. He hurried down toward camp. Linda would eat Pat alive if she found out.

THE RUSTLING SOUND of a woman's skirts startled Pat. She quickly turned from the cook stove and tensed when she saw a very pretty woman with golden-red hair. Her dress was a beautiful shade of blue, and Pat had never seen so much lace before.

"You there, I would like some coffee."

Pat nodded. "Sure thing. Have a seat and I'll bring it. I have some bread if you're hungry."

"Coffee is fine."

She looked as though she glided across the floor instead

of walked like everyone else. Pat watched, amazed, for a moment before she poured the coffee.

She set the cup down on the table. "Here ya go. I'm Pat, the cook."

"I'm Miss George, call me Linda. You wouldn't happen to know where my fiancé is, would you?"

Linda's flawless skin mesmerized Pat. It was so white, as though she never stepped into the sun. "What's his name?"

Linda smiled. "Samuel. I've been waiting forever for him to come down off this mountain. I'm tired of waiting, so here I am. I bet he'll be surprised."

"I think that's a safe bet." Pat smiled and turned away. Samuel had never mentioned a woman before, but they weren't confidants. She could only hope that the wagon had enough supplies to finish the cabin. She had work to do, so she'd have to check later. Maybe Fred could move her things back into the tent.

"Darling, there you are!"

Pat turned and watched as Linda hurried to the door and flung herself into Samuel's arms. She felt gut kicked and didn't know why. Linda was a lucky girl. Pat hid a smile behind her hand when she realized Samuel wasn't returning the embrace, and he wore a big frown. His gaze met hers, and her mirth knew no bounds.

Coughing to cover her laughter, she flew by them and went out the door. Things were going to be interesting around here. No wonder he never mentioned his lady. He didn't seem to know he had a fiancée. The men would have their eyes on Linda now. So much for the no women in the camp rule. She'd have no one to tell her she stank. Linda had brought her freedom.

Whistling, she went back into the cookhouse and promptly returned to the cook stove. She had pounds and pounds of pork chops to fry. Her heart tugged. Pork chops had been her

Da's favorite. Now, if you asked her, they were more like shoe leather than actual meat, but the men liked them.

The back of her neck tingled, and she knew someone was watching her. She turned slowly and discovered it was Samuel. He was standing just on the other side of the serving table. "Did you need something, boss?"

"I'll pack your things. You and I are moving into your cabin. Fred and Hank are putting up the cots, and Big Hans is installing the stove your father bought."

"What about a roof?"

"I thought we could stretch the wagon canvas over part of it for now. It shouldn't take a few of the men long to get it done."

So much for living by herself but she couldn't complain. Her cabin was being built. "You'll be staying until the wedding?"

His Adam's apple bobbed and he appeared decidedly uncomfortable. "I know we don't know each other very well, but people telling me what to do chaps my… I don't like it."

"I'm sorry. I never meant—"

"It's not you, Pat. My parents, her parents, and Linda have all decided my fate for me. I refuse to cow down to their dictates. I'm my own man, and I make my own decisions." He shrugged. "I just need to make sure never to be alone with her. I don't trust her, and I don't want to be leg shackled to her. I've given it some thought, and I think it best that you stick with me when you're not working. A type of chaperone. We'll get you cleaned up again so she can't object."

"No one will give me a second look while she's around."

"Exactly." Samuel smiled. "I'll let you get back to work. Smells great. Linda will be sitting at my table."

"Sure thing, boss." Pat nodded and her heart dropped when he left. She'd never cared what men thought of her before. It was true Linda was as pretty as the tallest pines, and the men would only have eyes for her. Somehow, though, hearing Samuel say it stung.

It was going to be a long fall and an even longer winter. She had more than enough to keep her busy. There was canning that needed to be done, sooner rather than later. Her and her da had spent all summer canning fruit and early vegetables. With the arrival of the supply wagon had come more vegetables to can.

Sighing, she went back to cooking. She had a heap of work to do, and it looked like a bath was in her future. What would it be like to not have to rub dirt on her face? As long as it didn't give away her secret, she was all for it.

GOOD LORD, but Linda could prattle on about the most mundane things. He'd tuned her out halfway through dinner. She was talking about his family and he really didn't care. They had their agenda, and he wanted no part of it. But he was stuck with Linda, and he'd have to find her a job to do. There was no living for free at the company camp, no exceptions.

He dreaded the squawking that was bound to happen when he brought up the subject. Maybe she could knit socks for the men or something. He'd talk to her about it after supper. His gaze returned again and again to Pat. For a tiny woman she sure did a lot of work. Maybe it was too much for her. He had never thought to ask her.

With her father living, there had been two cooks, and now she shouldered the burden alone. For now, there would be no help for it. He couldn't risk the men finding out she was female. He'd talk to her later when they were alone. His eagerness to be alone with her to talk took him by surprise. But then again she didn't prattle on.

"Right, Samuel?" Linda narrowed her eyes at him.

Damn, she knew he wasn't listening. "What was that? I'm sorry I was thinking about where we would cut next."

"I was saying that the men needed to clean up a bit. These awful beards must go. It's so uncivilized."

Leon, Fred, and Hank all smiled.

"We don't tell a man how to dress or groom up here. The work is extremely hard. Besides, up here we don't have to be part of society. This is what being a lumberjack is all about. Heck, if we asked them to shave we'd have a riot." Samuel saw her scowl, but he ignored it.

"After dinner I want to take a look at your arm. You must be suffering," she said as she gave him a doting smile.

"Not necessary. Pat takes care of it." He stared at his meal. He didn't want to see her scowl again.

"Oh?"

Leon nodded. "Pat and his pa knew a lot about healing with herbs and all."

"Herbs? You mean plants? Samuel, we are going to town in the morning. You need to see a proper doctor with proper medicine."

"Linda, I don't like being fussed over. Pat is doing a fine job, so let's just leave it at that. Besides, it's almost all healed. I'm just glad I didn't lose the hand." He felt a twinge of guilt at the satisfaction he got from how pale she became.

"Well, yes. Thank God for that. Really Samuel, this is the very reason you should be home where you belong." She daintily dabbed at her mouth with a napkin. "I'm ready; you can escort me home now."

"Fred, will you go and make sure the fire is lit as well as a lamp. I'll have Pat save you a piece of pie."

Fred immediately stood. "I'm holding you to that." He smiled and then left.

"Linda, my day extends well into the night. Paperwork needs to be done among other things. I have a feeling this visit will disappoint you. I don't have a lot of free time."

"Well, of course you work hard. Once we're married you can eat in our cabin."

He cocked his left brow. "You learned how to cook? That's a fine achievement."

Her face turned red. "I was thinking we could have Pat deliver our food to us."

Hank laughed. "I've never known a company cook to deliver before. I'm surprised Pat can keep up with feeding all the men."

"There are hours between each meal. I doubt it's a big problem." Linda patted her hair and looked around. "It's very efficient and I'm sure he has a lot of free time."

"I wouldn't know about that, Miss Linda," Leon said. "The dishes need to be washed and he's cooking for over twenty-five men. That's at least one hundred biscuits every morning. Plus at least seventy-five eggs and more than seven pounds of bacon. So, it's no easy job. He really could use some help if you ask me."

Her eyes widened. "Don't look at me. I'm a guest." She gave Samuel a sweet smile.

"We'll figure out something for you to do," Samuel said. "Leon, would you mind escorting Miss Linda to the cabin?"

"Aren't you going to take me?"

"I just don't have the time right now. Plus I have a no-women rule, and I can't be seen at the cabin. It would look like I was breaking the rule. Happy workers are the best workers. I will see you in the morning." He stood and pulled her chair back for her well aware every eye was upon him. "Have a good night."

"But what if I need something? Where will you be?"

"In a half built cabin down the hill from you. Listen, Hank and Leon's cabin is right next door. Just shout out and they'll be there. They can come get me if needed."

"You are pawning me off to the help?" She crossed her arms in front of her and stared at him. "Well?"

"I didn't know you were coming. I can't just drop everything and be at your beck and call. I'll stop by and get you for breakfast. Breakfast is before sun up."

Her mouth made a grim line. Giving him a curt nod, she lifted her head high and walked out of the cookhouse.

Every man had stopped eating and stared at him. It was always best to head off trouble. "Men, I suppose you've noticed Miss Linda George." There was laughter. "I still abide by my no women rule but I don't have much of a choice. It's too risky to send her down the mountain this time of year. I had no idea she was coming. I expect you all to show her the proper respect."

"You gettin' married?" one of the men shouted out.

"I never plan to tie myself to a woman, but if I do it'll be my choice. I think every man here agrees that they don't like to be told what to do in their private lives. My *father* thinks we should wed."

"She sure is pretty."

"Nope, you can't allow anyone to tell you what to do!"

"Stand up to your old man!"

"I'll take her!"

The last shout turned his blood cold. Damn, he'd have to assign her protection. "Like I said, she is to be respected by everyone." He hardened his voice. "I don't want any trouble, and I certainly don't want to have to fire anyone and send him down the mountain." He panned the crowd trying to make eye contact with as many as possible. An uneasy feeling gripped him.

"Pies are ready!" Pat called out as she dished out pieces as fast as possible. The men seemed to forget about Linda and focused on their mixed berry pie.

Sitting back down, Samuel sought out Pat's gaze and gave her a quick nod of thanks. If her secret came out, the men just might lynch him. How two women could be so different he didn't know. One wanted to work hard and keep to herself while the other craved attention and expected to be waited on. The image of Pat naked in his tub had played over and over in his head ever since he found her. It was hard to think of her as just a roommate. That was the very reason for his rule.

CHAPTER FIVE

*P*at finished the dishes, but she wasn't in any hurry to go to the cabin. Feelings she didn't recognize plagued her, and she wasn't sure what to think. For the first time, she wished she had a pretty dress to wear. She wanted to take her bindings off and be a real woman. Linda was now in camp. Certainly, another woman wouldn't make a difference. She didn't have anything to wear anyway. Besides, it would be considered scandalous that she'd been living with Samuel. It was a bit disheartening, but she needed to protect him from gossip. She pushed her wishes aside and dried her hands.

Taking a lantern, she walked down the path to her cabin. She opened the door and there was Samuel sitting by the woodstove.

He looked up when she entered and gave her a heart-stopping smile. "Good you're home. I know you hate it, but I have water heating for you."

His use of the word home warmed her beyond measure. "I don't hate it. It's just a disguise I need to keep hiding behind. I like being clean as much as the next person." She nodded and walked past him to the cot with her things on top. "I have some clean clothes to wear."

Samuel pulled the tub in front of the stove with one arm and added hot water to it and then splashed in some cold water. "There's a towel and soap on the chair."

"Thank you." She grabbed her clothes and laid them across the chair back. "Knock before coming in?"

He appeared very uncomfortable. "You see, the thing is I made a big deal about paperwork. I can't leave here. I bet Linda is watching the cabin right now."

"Oh, for heaven's sake. Sit at the table with your back to me. If I catch you peeking, I will poke your eye out." She waited for him to oblige before she turned her back and undressed. Her body tingled knowing he was but feet from her. Stepping into the tub, she yelped. The water was too hot. She grabbed the bucket of cold water and added more. She didn't need or want to turn around. She could feel the heat of his gaze upon her. It excited her to a point she felt wicked.

He didn't make a sound but she knew he still watched. With her back to him, there wasn't much for him to see as she sank into the clean water. In delight, she grabbed the soap and scrubbed every speck of dirt off her body. Being clean had been a luxury, and now she'd be able to keep clean. She still didn't know how she was going to keep up her disguise as a boy with a clean face.

Her breasts ached, both from being bound and because when she thought about Samuel, her nipples hardened. What was happening to her? She'd never known yearning for a man before, and she didn't like it. She shook her head as she shampooed her hair. No, that wasn't true. She liked it too much, and she sure didn't know what to do about it. He claimed he didn't like Linda but she was probably the type of woman he liked. Feminine, with big breasts and a pretty face.

Rinsing her hair, Pat bemoaned the fact that it was short.

Maybe it was time to let it grow out a bit. Many of the men had long hair. She shrugged. It wouldn't matter. He'd shown no interest in her except he didn't want to get caught having a female in camp. She could easily tell the men the truth, but she knew there'd be nothing but trouble after that. They'd look at her as a woman who could warm their beds.

Her Da had been right. The only way to stay safe was to be a man.

"Did you fall asleep again?"

Jarred out of her musings, she grabbed her towel. "I was just getting out." She stood and glanced over her shoulder. He had his back to her. Good, she could get dressed in peace. After she quickly dressed, she stood in front of the stove to warm up.

"Thank you for being a gentleman."

He turned and stared at her. "I still can't believe I thought you a boy. Your blonde hair is lovely." Shaking his head, he smiled. Then he dragged the tub out of the cabin to empty it. When he came back in, he wasn't alone. Linda hung onto his arm.

"Hi, Pat. I hope you don't mind leaving for a while. I have something I need to talk to Samuel about." She stared as though expecting Pat to skedaddle.

"I was just about to get some shut-eye. I need to be up a few hours before the sun."

Linda squeezed Samuel's arm. "You don't mind a late breakfast, do you?"

Samuel skillfully disentangled himself from Linda's hold. "Do you want a mob of hungry loggers wanting to lynch Pat? Sorry, but if you need something we can step out onto the porch and let Pat get his sleep."

Linda gave Pat a cold stare, shrugged her shoulders, and proceeded to walk outside. She looked back as though to be sure that Samuel was following.

Maybe they were really engaged after all. Linda seemed to think she had every right to just show up at his cabin. Thank God, she hadn't come any earlier or she'd have been shocked. It was a serious matter, but Pat couldn't help but chuckle. Lying down on her cot, she tried to sleep but she couldn't stop wondering what they were doing out on the porch.

"IF WE GOT MARRIED, we could share your cabin," Linda purred as she pressed her breasts against his good arm. "You wouldn't have to share with that boy."

"Pat's a good fella. I don't mind. Besides, I never asked you to marry me."

Linda gasped. "Our fathers agreed to the marriage. I consider that binding, as should you. I grew tired of waiting for you to come down off this mountain. Do you really think living in these primitive conditions suits me? No, I came because of you."

Samuel furrowed his brow as he took his arm back again. "Just where do you think we'd live if we married? This is it, this is as good as it gets. This is my home."

"Grow up, Samuel. It's time for you to live in town and take your place in the company. Being the owner has benefits, and we should enjoy them. Just think of the big house we can build. We'd be able to lord it over the ruffians down there."

The excitement in her voice nauseated him. Lord it over the ruffians? He hadn't realized just how selfish she was. "My cabin must have been a big letdown for you. Didn't you realize that you're here for the whole winter?"

Her eyes grew wide. "No, I'm not. I'm here to bring you back with me so we can be married."

"Who told you I'd be willing to go back with you?" His voice was gruffer than he intended.

"My father. He told me to come up here, and you'd have no choice but to marry me." She took a step closer to him. "You know you want me. You know you care for me. Come let's go back to your cabin. It'll be fine since we're to be married. In the morning we can go home." She gave him a great big smile.

"It's too dangerous to go back down now. If we hit snow, we'd be in big trouble. No more supply runs until there is plenty of snow and we use the sleighs. Even then it's dangerous and only the most seasoned of men go."

"It was beautiful coming up here. I love the colors of fall. The yellows, oranges, reds, all mixed together. Snow won't happen for at least a month, maybe two."

"I'm not going to argue with you. My word is law up here. Leon!" He knew Leon wasn't far since he was supposed to be guarding Linda tonight.

Leon stepped out of the shadows and nodded to Samuel. "I got it, boss. Miss George, it's time to get you back. The days in a logging camp are long, and we all need our rest."

"This isn't over, Samuel. I will talk to you in the morning." She turned on one heel and strode away. Then she sped up, and it was funny to watch Leon try to walk side by side with her. She was determined that he walk behind.

Samuel ran his hand over his face. His beard was beginning to fill in. He was surprised Linda hadn't commented on it. But he couldn't shave one-handed, and he simply refused to allow anyone else to use a sharp blade on his face. He was tired, but hopefully Pat would be awake to help him with his shirt. He'd learned to put his pants on by himself, and he could unbutton his shirt with one hand but getting the garment off gave him trouble.

He took a deep breath of the fragrant pine air. He'd

looked his full of Pat's naked backside. Her rear-end was heart shaped, and the gentle curve of her back was so grace-ful, he wanted to trace her spine with his tongue. Her hair was short enough he could see her neck. He could imagine himself nibbling on the back of her neck as his hands slid across her belly.

Damn, he was aroused again.

He couldn't very well ask her to rub dirt on herself again. He'd have to master some control over himself, or he'd end up embarrassed by his body's reaction to her. The heck with it, he could sleep in his shirt tonight.

He opened the door, expecting Pat to be in bed. Instead, she sat near the stove with tears rolling down her face.

His heart went out to her as he closed the door behind him. He crossed the room and knelt before her. "What happened?"

She sniffed and shook her head. "It's silly, really. I was looking through some of the crates my father ordered, and I found rose-scented soap, knitting needles and yarn. He made me get rid of my needles before we came up here. He knew we'd be living in a tent, and he didn't want anyone seeing me knit. He also bought me a few books, a nightgown and a skirt. He's not even here for me to thank him. He shouldn't have spent money on me." Tears rolled down her face. "I've been so busy that I've hardly had time to think of him as being gone. I guess I'll get the cabin done, and then in the spring I can go down the mountain and find work."

He placed his hand on her wet cheek, cupping it. "You don't have to worry. I'll protect you. No matter how gruff your father could be, he was always gentle with you. You were his pride. I could see it in his eyes when he gazed at you. You were blessed to have such a fine man as your father." Wetness clung to his thumb as he used it to wipe away a tear. She trembled as he slid his palm over her shoulder and down her arm to capture her hand. Then he stood, drawing her up with him. "Come on. It's time to get some sleep."

She swallowed hard as she gazed up at him. Then she nodded. "Yes, morning comes fast. Here let me help you with your shirt."

It was on the tip of his tongue to tell her to stop, but he enjoyed the closeness they shared. Her hands sent chills up his body each time she accidently touched his chest. If she knew what he was feeling, she'd probably run down the mountain and never look back.

"Thank you," His hand shook slightly as he took his shirt from her. The look of appreciation on her face as she stared at his chest almost made him groan. He quickly turned away. "Good night."

"Good night," she said softly.

A shiver rolled over him as he waited for her to get into her cot. Then he blew out the lamp and crawled into his bed. He was full of yearning. He'd had his share of women but none had ever had the effect on him that she did.

CHAPTER SIX

*W*hat a morning! Pat shook her head and started washing dishes. All Samuel had done was frown at her while Linda glared. What the heck was wrong with those two? Whatever it was, Pat wanted no part of it.

The sound of a tin cup falling to the ground alerted her that she wasn't alone. Cautiously, she turned and came face to face with Linda. Her glare was even worse up close.

"Can I get you more coffee?"

"No, you can't get me more coffee. I know all about you. You disgust me, and I want you out of Samuel's cabin this instant. In fact, the farther away you go the better. I'd better not see you looking at him ever again." The angry contortions of her face were frightening.

"I'm sure I don't know what you mean." Pat stared back trying to act brave while her heart pounded painfully against her chest. "If you have a problem, I'm sure Samuel is the one to talk to." She turned back to the washtub.

"You know I always wondered why Samuel had a no-women rule but now with the truth out, I'm sickened by you.

Now, pack your things. Hans said he'd personally take you to town."

What was she talking about? Slowly Pat turned. "I have a job here. You have no call to tell me to leave. Even if you did, I'm not going anywhere with Big Hans. Do you have any idea what he'll do to me?"

Linda laughed. "The same thing every other man has been doing with you. I've heard about boys like you. Now get going and pack a bag!"

Pat felt frozen to the spot she stood. Her mind whirled. "Where is Samuel?"

"Not here. There's no one to save you." Linda laughed and grabbed a knife off the table. "I said to go."

Pat nodded. "Sure, I'll go." She backed away until she was at the door. She opened it, intending to run but Big Hans caught her and lifted her up over his shoulder. He had a pack mule ready. He grabbed the reins and turned toward the cookhouse. "Remember Miss, not a word to anyone. If anyone asks, I went hunting and will be back in a few days."

"Thank you," Linda said.

Pat started to kick and before she got out a scream, she was slammed to the ground and hit on the head.

The next thing she knew she was lying face down on the back of a mule. Her head hurt and she was sick to her stomach. "Ouch," she cried.

"Yell all ya want, boy. We're far enough out no one will hear us. Ain't no one heading this way. They think we're going down the mountain. What they don't know is I found a way to the other side of the mountain." Hans pulled on the reins. "Git going, you good for nothing mule."

As much as being on the mule hurt, Pat didn't want to stop. As long as they were moving, he wasn't touching her. What would he do when he found out she was a woman? The only hope she had was to pray.

"WHAT DO you mean there's no food cooked?" Anger filled Samuel only to be replaced by concern. He'd been at the cutting site most of the day. "Did anyone check the cabin for Pat?"

Hank nodded. "I looked everywhere. I even checked the area he likes to go to pick his plants. I can't find him. Strange, really. I've never known the boy to wander far from camp."

"Me neither," Samuel said before he started to run down the road toward camp. Something was horribly wrong, he could feel it. Pat wouldn't go anywhere without letting him know. Where could she be?

A crowd had gathered in front of the cookhouse and most of the men were grumbling.

"Have any of you looked for Pat?"

There was a lot of shifting and shrugging going on. "Fan out. I want him found."

Most of the men started to walk down the road toward the cutting.

"Fan out! That means go in different directions. Some down, some up, some toward the road, some away from the road." He'd never noticed just how dense a lot of the men were. He watched as they finally spread out and began to look. Leon came hurrying to his side.

"Pat is missing? I haven't seen Big Hans in hours. I was just about to let you know when I heard Pat was gone. You don't think—"

"That's exactly what I think. Someone must have seen something. Who was in camp most of the day?"

"Besides Pat, there was Miss Linda and Old Barney. Old Barney has been feeling a mite poorly lately, and I told him to stay in bed. Pat was going to look in on him after breakfast." Leon said.

"Let's go and talk to Barney. Hank, find Miss Linda and have her come to the cookhouse. I'm assuming she's still in camp."

"Yes, she is, boss. I'll get her right away." Hank hurried away.

Samuel hastened to the cabin that housed Barney and a few others. He didn't bother to knock, just walked right in. The air was foul with sickness and waste. "Still feeling poorly?"

Barney nodded. "I am."

"Sorry to hear that. Listen, did Pat ever stop by to check on you?" Samuel asked, trying to be patient.

"No, he didn't. But I heard a heck of a lot of meanness coming from Miss Linda. She told Pat to leave. Something about you and him." Barney said each word slowly. "I think Big Hans offered to take Pat to town. I thought maybe it was a dream or something."

"Thanks, Barney. I'll send someone in to tend to you."

"Thank you, boss. Hope you find that young 'un."

Samuel hurried out of the cabin and ran to the cookhouse. He slammed open the door and took a menacing step toward Linda. "How dare you tell any of my workers they can leave? How dare you order Pat off the mountain? Now where are they?" he thundered.

Linda put a shaking hand to her chest. "I was just saving you from yourself. I know all about the affection you and Pat share. A man cleaves to his wife and only his wife."

"What goes on in this camp is none of your business. What I do is none of your business! Which way did Big Hans go? You'd better tell the truth, or I'll put you out!"

"So it's true! You care for Pat." Linda sat down in a chair and her shoulders slumped. Tears filled her eyes. "Hans said he knew of a secret way to get to the other side of the mountain. He said no one has been there before."

"Pompous ass. I know every inch of my mountain. Yes, Linda, my mountain. My father might own the saw mill, but I own the land." He marched back out the building. "Leon! I need you to stay here. You're in charge. Hank and Fred grab some firearms. We're going after Pat. Oh, Leon, make sure someone tends to Barney and cleans out that cabin."

He didn't wait for an answer. He hurried to Pat's cabin and grabbed his bedroll along with his canteen and some food. He always had the bag ready. The forest could be a dangerous place. As he walked out of the cabin, he met up with Fred and Hank. He grabbed his gun and off they went.

"We headed to Pearse's Point?" Fred asked.

"Indeed we are. We'd best hurry. Pat is in grave danger." He took long, quick strides across the forest floor. There were places where the trees were so dense, the sun barely came though.

At one point, Samuel held up his hand, signaling for the other two to hold their positions. He squatted down and stared at the earth. "We're on their trail, and so is our friend, Ford." He took a deep breath and let it out slowly. Then he turned toward the two men. "Pat will be fine. Ford gets a bit testy when someone is kidnapped. He himself was caught by the French Military and turned into an unpaid soldier. Ford escaped, but he still lives in these woods. Come on. When Hans finds out Pat is a girl well, I don't know how he'll react. He might just kill her."

"Boss? What did you mean about Pat being a girl?" Hank asked. His confusion was clear in his voice.

He sighed. Damn his big mouth! "Long story. Her father didn't want any of the loggers going after his daughter, so he disguised her as a boy to keep her safe." He turned away and walked on, not willing to answer any more questions. His urgency to get to Pat became overpowering. He'd make it before sundown, and he could only pray she would be spared. The thought of her being in danger twisted his stomach, and bile rose in his throat. Damn Linda, and damn Hans to hell and back. What right did they have to decide another's fate?

He ran when the path was clear and became more cautious when the foliage was dense. He'd lost sight of Fred and Hank, but he knew they were behind him and would be there to help. He'd heard a story of what Big Hans had done to a boy, but he'd thought it to be tall tale. Now he wasn't so sure. He should have protected Pat.

Familiar landmarks told him he was almost there. He dropped his things, all except for his knife and gun. He'd be at a disadvantage with his arm but he was quicker than Hans. Drawing a deep breath, he tried to calm himself. Going in with emotions high would be a mistake. He couldn't afford the tiniest of mistakes.

With one knee on the ground, he panned the area, spotting a flickering light in the distance. Hans was so confident no one had been to this spot he didn't hide his fire. Slowly, Samuel looked in the woods surrounding Hans and Pat. He finally spotted Ford. Only because he knew the other man would be there, was Samuel able to spot him. Ford was good, very good. Slowly Samuel backtracked until he caught Fred and Hank. He filled them in, and they took up positions.

———

PAT'S NAUSEA disappeared as she became more and more frightened. She shuddered as Hans described what he had planned for the boy, Pat. What would he do when he found out the truth? No one would ever know what happened to her. Samuel would never know how she felt about him. Her heart broke. Boy, girl, it didn't matter. No one would want her if she survived. She'd never know the pleasure of Samuel's embrace or feel his lips on hers.

Her only comfort was she'd be reunited with her Mother and Da. They'd be at heaven's gate to greet her. She hadn't a long life, but it had been a good life. She'd seen enough misery in her lifetime to know how lucky she'd been. Maybe throwing herself off a cliff would be better than what Hans had planned.

She yelped when Hans kicked her side.

"Are you payin' attention to me, boy? Maybe I should slice your skin off patch by patch. I bet you'd scream nice and loud. You'll be begging me to stop." He grabbed a knife from his belt and waved the blade around. "I've never skinned a human alive before." His smile was evil.

Pat swallowed hard. All he'd done so far was slapped her around, kicked her, and told her what he was going to do. It was as though talking about his plan for her made him euphoric. She tried to stay quiet. Now she needed to remain focused on what he had to say. Once he stopped talking, she feared the worst.

Hans reached down and grabbed her by the arm. He dragged her to the nearest tree. She kicked out hitting his leg. He slapped her so hard in the face she almost passed out. Blood trickled from her nose. He sat her up against the tree and tied her to it.

She'd never felt so much pain and her eyes teared.

"A sissy boy. Too bad you'll never live to become a man." The menace in his voice was more than frightening.

Every bad word she'd ever heard crossed her thoughts, but she didn't dare utter them. Breathing became labored, and she feared her ribs were broken. Hopelessness engulfed her as she watched him smile in triumph. The excruciating pain she felt now was probably nothing compared to the agony she'd feel soon enough. She didn't have any expectations of being rescued. Who would rescue her? Perhaps Samuel, but he wouldn't miss her for long. He had his fiancée waiting for him in camp. He'd have a life of wretchedness if he married Linda. Too bad he didn't know her true nature. He claimed to not want Linda, but who could resist her pretty smile for long?

"Sit tight. I'm going to gather wood for a fire. I've decided to keep you a few days before I kill you. I want to relish our time together."

"They'll miss you at camp."

"Naw. I figure with you fightin' me I'll have a few scratches on me. I'll spin a yarn of tangling with some varmint." He laughed and wagged his finger at her. "Don't go nowhere."

As soon as he was out of sight, she frantically struggled to get free, but it was useless. She could hardly breathe. Terror left her cold and shaking. Her heart filled with what-ifs. Perhaps she should have lived her life as a woman. She should have gotten off the mountain as soon as her father died. It was too late now, but that was all she could think of.

She heard a yelp and a crashing in the forest. Big Hans probably tripped over a log. He'd be extra ornery when he got back. She slumped back against the tree as her heart beat faster. She was exhausted but fear kept her alert.

Footsteps rustled through the bushes behind her, and she wished she could be brave.

"Shh. Honey, it's me." Samuel said as he cut the rope that bound her.

Surely, she was dreaming. Her fright was making her see things.

Samuel rounded the massive tree and knelt before her. Her eyes grew wide and she quickly shut them. It wasn't possible. He was still there when she opened them again. Reaching out she touched him.

"He's going to kill me. Run while you can," she told him.

"He's dead. You don't need to worry about him again." He reached out to touch her arm but she jerked away.

"Don't touch me!" She shied away, wrapped her arms around her ribs and groaned in pain. She couldn't help it. She didn't want anyone to put their hands on her. Why didn't she feel relieved? She'd hoped to be saved but somehow she still didn't feel safe.

Hank, Fred, and a big man wearing a raccoon hat and buckskins entered the camp. "We got him," the big man said. "You must be Pat. I'm Ford. I live near abouts. Glad you're safe."

Her heart sped up at the sheer size of the man. She gave him a quick nod and looked away. She wanted to be left alone. The anguish in her heart was unbearable, and her throbbing body hurt little in comparison. What would she do now? She couldn't stay in camp. Her unknown fate terrified her.

"Can you stand?" Samuel asked gently.

She nodded and tried shaking off all offers of help. Finally, she got up on her own and leaned back against the tree. She could hardly take in a deep enough breath. "Let's go." She pushed off from the tree and almost fell face first. Samuel righted her but she shrugged his hands off her again. "It'll be dark soon." Wincing with each step, she walked in the direction she had come. She took slow shallow breaths and concentrated on putting one foot in front of the other.

She took note of the concern on all the men's faces but she wanted to put space between her and the spot Big Hans had brought her to. She trudged on until a fallen tree trunk stood in her way. Tears fell as she realized she wouldn't be able to climb over it. She was broken inside and out. Finally, she walked around it. Even her thinking was slow.

Turning back to the men, she sighed. "You all go back to

camp. I'm not going to make it before nightfall. I'm sorry, I won't be able to cook today. Perhaps tomorrow…" She stared down at her feet.

"Ma'am, are you planning to stay out here alone?" Ford's face scrunched with concern.

"Are you sure he's dead?" she whispered.

"Yes, ma'am."

"Did they tell you I'm a woman?"

"Tell me? Why would they need to do that?" Ford scratched his head. "It's as plain as the day is long."

She turned to Fred and Hank. "Did you know?"

"Not until today," Hank answered.

"So, everyone knows?"

Fred shook his head. "Not that I know of."

"I've rested enough. Let's continue," she said taking a shaky step.

Samuel cleared his voice. "You men go on back. I'll stay with Pat and see that she's up to traveling in the next few days. It looks as though there's enough supplies on this old mule. I only have one thing to ask. Please don't tell anyone Pat's a she."

"My lips are sealed," Fred said.

"Mine too, boss." Hank nodded in agreement.

"Don't worry about me," Ford said. "I don't like to talk no how. You take care of her. Her body and soul both need tending." Before anyone was able to say goodbye, Ford disappeared into the woods.

"Take your time, boss. We got you covered. Old Cappin can cook for a few days," Hank said. Both Hank and Fred nodded to her before they left.

Pat simply waited until they were out of sight before she crumpled to the ground.

CHAPTER SEVEN

*S*amuel's heart ached for Pat. The whole ordeal had stolen her happiness and her will. It was as though she didn't care what happened to her now. He found a spot for them to camp and made a fire. He helped her to sit and all she'd done for the last two hours was stare at the dancing flames. He understood her need to be alone, so he didn't prod her. Better to let her be.

Darkness had fallen, but they couldn't see the stars in the dense woods. What would she think if he told her he owned all of the land for as far as they could see? She probably wouldn't care. He handed her another damp cloth for her to hold against her cheek. She already had a black eye, and he feared her nose was broken. It looked to be out of place. Fixing it would just cause more pain.

"Pat, your nose is a bit crooked. Honey, I think it's broken, and I can straighten it for you, but it's going to hurt like hell."

Reaching up, she tenderly touched her nose. Wincing, she nodded. "I may have need of a husband someday. It'll be easier to find one if my nose isn't crooked." The slight smile she gave him was in stark contrast to the pain in her eyes.

He stoked her hair and nodded. Reaching out, he settled his fingers against her nose then pushed it back into place. It hurt his heart when she screamed. "I'm so sorry, Pat. It's done."

He stood and grabbed the saddlebags the mule had been carrying. He rummaged through them until he found what he was looking for. Then he hurried back to her with the bottle of whiskey. "You probably haven't had much experience drinking, but a little bit can help with the pain."

"No, I need to keep my wits about me. My Da always told me that it could be the only advantage I had." Tears pooled in her lovely eyes and spilled down her face. "I never meant to cause you so much trouble. You should go back to camp. Linda is there waiting for you."

"She's the one who sent you away."

"Yes, I know, but only because she loves you. She thought you to be involved with me or rather the boy, Pat. She doesn't know you very well, does she?"

"Why do you say that?"

"I've never seen you looking at men that way. I have seen you trying to peek at me though." The ends of her mouth turned up before she winced.

"She's a spoiled brat who wants things no matter who gets hurt. I haven't told you much about myself. You see, I've always been a bit of a wanderer. Much like your father. I worked the gold mines and got lucky; extremely lucky. I own this mountain and all its timber."

"I thought you were the foreman."

"I am the foreman *and* the owner. I brought my father out here to run the sawmill. He's made a fair chunk of money, and he owns a lot of the town. I don't interfere with him, and he wasn't supposed to interfere with me. Somewhere about a year ago, he found himself a partner. The partner is Linda's father. They all became greedy and decided if I married Linda it would give them a piece of the mountain. I ignored the whole thing until now. What they don't understand is, I don't need them. I can build my own sawmill and my own town. A town that doesn't swindle people with high prices. A town where there aren't more saloons than houses. A town that has a lawman to keep the citizens safe."

"That's a nice dream to have. I know you'll get it accomplished."

"If you weren't so hurt right now I'd kiss you." He waited for a reaction from her but there wasn't one. "I don't want the other men to know I own the mountain."

"Why?"

"They'd treat me differently. No one ever likes the owner."

"You might be right about that. I won't tell."

"Do you want to talk about what happened today? Don't answer now. I'll build a fire and then we can talk." He stood and began gathering wood. Using his ax, he chopped enough for the night. It did some good to swing his ax. It got some of his anger out. He wanted to be as gentle as possible around Pat.

"I can only imagine how bad I look," she said when he piled the wood near the spot he picked to make a fire.

"You'll always look beautiful to me."

Her eyes briefly brightened before they filled with pain. "Thank you. You lie, but thank you. I need you to tend to my ribs. They are worse than I thought, and I'm going to have to take the binding off my…my…"

"I know where your bindings are." He sat next to her again. "I'm going to take your shirt off."

He lifted it up from the back, over her head and down her arms. The bruises on her made him gasp. They were so dark and angry. He knew firsthand how much bruises that deep in color hurt. Slowly he unwound the length of cloth that kept her breasts flattened. As he removed more and more, her cleavage was exposed, then most of her breasts came into view and then finally her rosy nipples. He couldn't help the arousal he felt.

"Oh boy, that feels so good to let them free. Use the same cloth to wrap my ribs please."

He knelt so he could get an even amount of pressure on each side. Her back was a mass of bruises too. If Hans hadn't already been dead, he'd go hunt him down and kill him. "I'm so sorry this happened to you. I knew Hans was dangerous, but I had no idea he'd do this."

"You didn't know. He always watched me, but I'm not sure he would have taken me out of camp if Linda hadn't told him to. I can't believe she loves you. She almost seems incapable of any tender feelings."

"Her love is not reciprocated."

"I know. You have no love for any woman."

He opened his mouth to deny her statement, but she put her finger over his lips.

"I don't want to talk about it anymore." The emotion in her voice shook him.

He accidently grazed the underside of her breasts as he wrapped her ribs. Her resulting shiver gave him hope. She wasn't completely immune to him.

"All done. Let's get your shirt back on."

She blushed as though she forgot she was exposed. "Thank you, Samuel. You've always been more than kind to me. It'll be sad to leave you when we get back to camp."

He furrowed his brow as he frowned. There would be no leaving but now wasn't the time to discuss it. "I have biscuits and beans for dinner. Then I think you should get some sleep. You've had quite the day."

SHE WATCHED as Samuel got the fire started. He put coffee on to boil and handed her a biscuit. She took it from him but ended up staring at it. Her stomach was in knots so tight there was no way she could eat. There wasn't a part of her body that didn't hurt. She knew it could be worse, much worse. But that didn't help the agony she now experienced. She felt afloat without an anchor. There was no place to hang her hat anymore. Selling the cabin wouldn't bring in much money and there was no way to know for certain she'd make it to town before it snowed.

The future was dire, and it hurt to think about it. It hurt to think about what had been done to her and what she'd been saved from. It was too much, and she felt herself shutting down. She'd miss Samuel something awful, and she couldn't face it.

He put the bedroll next to the fire and then he sat next to her. "Not hungry?"

"I can't seem to eat. My stomach is in knots." She kept her gaze on the biscuit in her hands.

"It's going to be a cooler night. Do you want to lie down?" His voice was so gentle it almost made her cry.

She groaned loudly as she stood up. "I need to…"

"Back behind that tree should be fine. I won't look."

She started to walk toward the tree but she looked back to be sure he was still there. She'd lost her grit and her courage. Life was so dang hard. After she was done, she went back to the camp and gingerly sat down on the bedroll.

"There's only one bedroll. Where are you going to sleep?"

Samuel gave her a reassuring smile. "Don't you worry. I'll just lean against this tree and keep watch over you."

Tears filled her eyes, but she refused to give into them,

afraid she'd never stop once she got started. She simply lay down and stared into the flames.

The next thing she knew, she was screaming and fighting off her attacker. Her heart beat so fast, surely it would pound its way out of her chest, but she refused to give up.

"Pat, it's me Samuel. You had a bad dream. It's all right. You're safe with me. Hans isn't here anymore. Honey, take a deep breath and let it out slowly."

It took a minute for her to focus on Samuel and understand what he was saying. The flames of the fire lit up his face, and she cringed. "I scratched you. I'm so sorry. I don't seem to know what's going on anymore."

He'd been on his knees, but now he lay behind her pulling her close enough to wrap his arms around her. It felt nice to be cocooned in his brawny arms. He murmured to her in a soothing tone, and eventually she relaxed enough to fall back to sleep.

In the morning, she found herself sprawled out on his chest. She almost gasped when she realized his chest was bare. If this was all she was ever to have, she wanted it to last as long as possible. Trying to stay still was hard. She ran her hands over his powerful chest, touching his dark hair. Her body hurt, but being here with him made her ache in a way she had never known.

He placed his hand over hers startling her before guiding it to his mouth. He kissed each of her fingers sending pleasure through her.

"My hands aren't those of a fine lady. They're red and calloused." She lifted her head and rested her chin on his chest.

He gazed at her with hooded eyes. "You think I mind? It just means you're a hard worker. It's not as though we're set up for tea parties up here."

"You have a point."

"It hurts me to look at you. The pain you're enduring must be horrific. If it was in my power I'd take all your pain away." He stroked her hair.

"You're very nice Samuel, but I don't need pity. Really, I don't. I think I'll be able to make it back to camp today. I'm taking you away from your work. I'm sure they found a replacement cook by now. And I need to get down off this mountain as soon as I can."

Samuel gazed at her quietly and finally he nodded. "I'll rustle up some breakfast then we can move on." He gently rolled her off him then cupped her cheek in his hand. "Things will be fine, you'll see."

She didn't know what he meant or what he looked for when he stared into her eyes. Whatever it was, she was sure he didn't get his answer. Yes, it was going to be hard to say goodbye to him. After she got to her feet, she tried stretching to see just how hurt she was. Her limbs all worked. Her face was a mess, and her ribs hurt like hell, but she'd make it. She might be small, but she was strong.

They ate a quick meal, and then Samuel packed everything up and loaded it onto the mule. As they started their walk, Samuel held the reins in one hand as she wrapped her hand around his bicep. Somehow being with him made everything a bit better. She'd pretend things were fine until she got to camp. What type of reception she'd receive, she didn't know. Her nerves stretched taut, and her pain increased as they got closer to camp.

She jerked her hand out of his. "Am I a boy or a woman?"

He stared at her breasts and sighed. "Come, let's get your breasts bound. I wish it could be different, but it's not."

"I understand." Her voice wobbled. Indeed, she did understand. Her moments of happiness with Samuel were over, and she needed to tuck all her feelings away in the corner of her heart. Maybe someday she'd take them back out and be able to relive how he valued her. How he looked at her the way a man gazed at a woman. How safe and blissful he made her feel. It was time for Pat the cook to reappear.

A chilled wind blew as he removed her shirt. He stared at her hardened nipples and there was no shame involved. She wanted him to look his fill. All too soon, he loosened the binding around her ribs and wrapped it around her breasts. He helped her back into her shirt and quickly glanced away. Her head understood, but her heart cried out to him.

She bent and picked up a handful of dirt.

"What are you doing?"

"I'm going to rub dirt on my face."

"It's not needed, Pat. You're badly bruised and your nose is so swollen, no one would mistake you for a girl." He held out his hand to her, but she pretended she didn't see it.

All closeness had to end. It was only sensible. She needed to remember not to make cow eyes at Samuel. "I'm ready. Let's get to camp. I'd like to go to my cabin and rest for a bit."

Samuel led the way into camp, and they were instantly surrounded by well-meaning loggers. One even slapped her on the back and blackness almost engulfed her.

"Stand back. Pat has had a time of it. Cracked ribs and a broken nose. I'm telling you, he's braver than most men I know."

The crowd parted for Pat the boy, and her heart shattered. So much for tucking her feelings away. It was too late now. She nodded at a few of the loggers until finally she was at her front door. She pushed it open and went right to her bunk. Too bad there wasn't a way to shut herself away.

Samuel closed and locked the door. "Let's get your ribs wrapped up again."

"I can do it myself."

"You tended to me. Besides, I've already seen you. It'll be

fine," he murmured. He cupped her cheek and gazed into her eyes. "What am I going to do with you?"

A knock on the door startled them both. "It's me, Linda. Let me in. I can tend to Pat."

Pat grabbed Samuel's arm. "I don't want her in here."

"Nor do I. I'll be right back." Samuel went out the front door and quickly closed it behind him.

She heard a loud noise and what sounded like an angry conversation, but she couldn't decipher what they were saying. Suddenly it was quiet, but Samuel didn't return. Slowly she stood and found one of her father's old shirts among her things. Next, she used a knife to cut it into strips of cloth. Finally, she sat on her cot and wrapped her ribs as tightly as she could. It hurt to breathe, it hurt to move. As soon as her head hit her pillow, she was asleep.

CHAPTER EIGHT

*S*amuel hit the side of the huge pine tree with his ax. He needed to get out his frustration before he blew up at people. Pat had barely looked at him in the week they'd been back, and Linda refused to leave him alone. His no-women rule was not being broken by one but by two cantankerous females.

He'd told Linda more than once to leave him be. The only time he could be totally free from her was to be deep in the forest with the other men. Pat seemed broken, and she wouldn't talk to him about it. It hurt that she refused to confide in him. It was agony lying on the cot next to her and not being free to reach out and touch her.

He swung his ax so hard he felt it all the way down to his toes. What had happened? He'd thought they were developing a relationship, but ever since they'd been back, she had pulled away and shut him out. She had insisted on going back to work that morning, and he could see she was in pain, but she wouldn't listen to him.

All she talked about was earning her keep. He suspected she'd rather be anywhere but on the mountain. *Stubborn little female!* Why couldn't she just accept his help? She had wrapped her own ribs. When he tried to help, she had flinched, and the hurt in her eyes was almost too much to bear.

Fall was still holding against winter, and she'd asked more than once to be taken down to town. He refused, and he forbade anyone to leave the mountain without his permission. Pat was still bruised, but she refused his help. How she was able to cook for all the men astounded him. She was a spitfire for sure.

Only a few of the men asked about Hans, but after a day they stopped looking. They figured he left; it wouldn't be the first time he'd done that to an outfit. Samuel stacked the wood near the now completed cabin he shared with Pat. It was especially hard to hear her undress each night. He ached to take her into his arms and make sweet love to her.

He chopped more wood until he heard horses headed his way. He took a wide stance, ax in hand waiting for the arrival. Frowning, he shook his head when he recognized not only his father but Linda's father too riding in a wagon. It was going to be a hell of a day.

The wagon came closer, and Samuel walked toward it with his ax still in hand. "Father, Mr. George." He nodded his head in greeting. "What the hell are you doing here?"

His father's face grew red while Mr. George stood in the wagon and almost lost his footing. "Now see here," Mr. George started. He grabbed the side of the wagon and then hopped down. "We're here to make sure you made an honest woman of my girl."

Samuel lifted his left brow. "Honest? Do any of you know what the word means?"

His father scrambled out of the wagon and stood next to Mr. George. "Show some respect, Samuel. We've come to make the wedding proper. This is—" He turned and helped an elderly gentleman from the wagon. "This is Reverend Pulley. He's here to marry you and Linda proper. We got worried when you didn't come back to town."

"Good day, Reverend. I'm sorry you've been sent on a folly of a ride. There will be no wedding. I'm surprised you chanced coming up this time of year."

"A folly?" The reverend turned and stared at his two travelers.

"Don't worry. Samuel knows what's expected, and he'll do the right thing." His father took a step closer to him. "Isn't that right, son?"

"I repeat, there will be no wedding. I never proposed to Linda, and I have no intention of doing so. Your best bet would be to take Linda back down with you, today." He was not about to be cornered by them.

"Daddy!" Linda came running out of the cabin and ran into her father's embrace. "It's been simply awful here. I'm so glad you've come. Samuel thinks nothing of taking what he wants. He ruined me and refuses to marry me."

She was up to no good again. Samuel glared at her. Out of the corner of his eye, he saw Pat hurry to their cabin. He didn't blame her for trying to stay out of the line of fire. If he could, he'd run in the other direction too.

He stared at Linda in exasperation. "You know full well I've never laid a hand on you. I'm not some stupid hick you can lead around by the nose." He stared at each of them in turn. "I'm not marrying Linda, and that's that. My suggestion is you turn around and leave, taking Linda with you. Unmarried women who spend time in the camps get a bad name. Now, I didn't invite any of you. Feel free to leave."

His father whirled on him. "Now see here. You need us to cut the timber. We can always find another supplier. You need to step in line and do as you're told."

Samuel took off his hat and ran his fingers over the brim,

trying to contain his temper. His decision to build his own town had been a good one. He just hadn't known he would have to act so quickly. "I'm not worried about it. I have the finest timber there is. It won't be hard to find another sawmill. You were mistaken in thinking I'd allow myself to be under your thumb."

Mr. George stepped forward. "I don't care about the bad blood between you and your father. My little girl is getting married today. You'd best get that through your thick head."

"Oh, really?"

PAT STARED at the skirt her father had bought her. She had a blouse she could wear with it. It wasn't elegant or considered proper by some but it was all she had. Samuel had been too good to her, and she wasn't about to allow him to be pushed into marrying that insane woman. Plus it would be revenge for Linda's part in Hans kidnapping her.

Maybe Samuel wouldn't want her help. Her hands shook as she undressed and unbound her plentiful breasts. He just might send her away too, but she needed to try to help him any way she could. Donning the skirt was easy enough. Her top gave her trouble. It was a bit tight around her chest and it was hard getting all the hooks closed. Taking off her hat, she wished her hair was a bit longer, but there was no help for it now. She brushed it until it gleamed and then admired herself in the mirror. It was the best she could do.

She walked to the door and her hand shook as she lifted the latch. This might be the biggest mistake of her life. It would be so easy to just stay out of the whole thing, but Samuel was her friend. She needed to help him.

Pulling her shoulders back, she opened the door and stepped outside. They were all in front of the cookhouse arguing. All except for the reverend had red mottled faces. She walked closer trying to be as graceful as she could. She didn't even have shoes on, but that fact was hidden by her skirt. Maybe she should have worn her boots.

No one took note of her as she walked toward them, until Linda caught sight of her. Linda's eyes grew wide, and her jaw dropped. The rest of the party all turned and stared.

Pat's face heated as she stayed on course. She kept her gaze on Samuel, wondering what he was thinking. So many emotions crossed his face from confusion, to awareness, and then to awe. He smiled wide, and when she was almost to them, he walked toward her and held out his arms for her to grab.

She smiled at him, searching his eyes for anger, but there wasn't any to be found. "I wasn't sure what else to do," she whispered.

"You are amazing."

He led her to the group and introduced her to everyone. Linda turned white and looked close to passing out.

"Pat, you're a woman?" Linda clutched her chest and walked into her father's arms.

"You have a camp woman?" Samuel's father clenched his hands into fists. "Who is this slut?"

Samuel dropped her hand and swung at his father. The sound of his fist hitting bone made Pat shudder, and she cried out when the older man fell to the ground. The reverend immediately went and helped the older man back to a standing position.

"Perhaps we should have this conversation in the cook-house. I can make coffee," Pat suggested. She didn't wait for a reply. She marched to the door and let herself in then hurried to the cook stove.

"Father, this is where Pat works. He, or rather she, pretended to be a boy the whole time she was here. I had no idea Samuel was living with a woman." Tears rolled down Linda's face.

If Linda hadn't been such a troublemaker, Pat might have felt sorry for her. But she didn't.

Pat poured the coffee, put all the cups on a tray and carried it to the table before she sat down next to Samuel. "Samuel just recently found out I was a woman. I've been living as a boy for as long as I can remember. My father moved around a lot, and he feared for my safety if the truth was known. We've been just about everywhere. Most recently, we panned for gold before coming here. He was the cook, and I helped. He died not too long ago. I kept up my disguise for the same reason he did. It was for my own safety."

Linda slammed her cup down on the table, splattering coffee in all directions. She narrowed her eyes and stared at Samuel. "You knew, and you didn't kick her out of your cabin? She's the reason you didn't have time for me? She's nothing but a dirty, filthy camp whore!"

Pat closed her mouth tight and clasped her hands in front of her. She was afraid of what she might say.

"She's not a whore. She's not filthy. She rubs dirt on herself to keep her disguise, but she's actually very clean. She's very resourceful. Her father died, but she worked her tail off and became one of the best camp cooks we've had. She cooks better than her father. She tended to me when I hurt my arm. She stitched me up. She has more courage than all of you put together. Have you forgotten how you gave Pat to Big Hans, Linda? You thought to be rid of Pat but she persevered. She was quick witted and she survived. She pulls her weight around here which is a heck of a lot more than I can say about you, Linda."

"I came here as you fiancée, not some work horse. There's a big difference. I bet she can't even read. I've waited far too long for you Samuel. We're getting married. Today."

"I'm carrying his child," Pat almost slapped her hands over her mouth. Where the heck had *that* come from?

Samuel didn't even look surprised. He nodded and put his arm around her. "That is the very reason you and I are not getting married, Linda. Pat and I are. I want my child to have my name."

Linda stood. "Just how many men have had you, Pat? It's convenient to tell Samuel the baby is his. You were alone with Hans for a long time before you were found. Why it could be any number of men's baby. You don't fool me."

Pat looked at Samuel, waiting for him to take the lead.

"Well, Reverend. I have to say I'm glad you're here. Will you officiate our wedding? Mine and Pat's? After all, it is the right thing to do."

At the reverend's nod, Linda shrieked and ran from the building. "I'll be back in an hour to perform the ceremony," the reverend said. All the rest of the men stood and shook their heads as they walked outside.

"An hour should give us enough time to get away for a bit. They'll be gone by the time we get back," Pat said as she tried to relax her tense body.

"We're not going anywhere. You and I are getting married."

"Heck, you don't even like me. Well, sometimes you do. I mean we're friends and all, but there is much more to marriage than that." Pat stood and gathered up the cups. "Besides, if we're not leaving I have some cooking to do."

"Why wouldn't I want to marry you?" His voice was so tender it hurt.

"I'm not good enough for you. Someone like Linda would be best for the owner of an outfit like this. I'd be an embarrassment to you. I'm not refined or cultured. I am a little bit educated, but I'm not for you." Her stomach tied in knots as her heart ached. "Tell them whatever you need to get them to leave. I'll have my own cabin, and come spring I can leave too."

Samuel lifted the tray of cups from her grasp and set it down. Taking both her hands in his he gave them a gentle squeeze as he gazed into her eyes and smiled. "Is that what you think? I want a woman who can plan parties and sit nicely at the opera? You are educated, Pat. You can read and write, and you have real world experience. I don't want a hothouse flower for a wife. I have no use for someone who isn't my equal. Together we can forge ahead and make a real town. A place where families will want to live. A place with schools and a real church. We can make it happen."

"You really want me for your wife?"

"Is that so hard to believe? You're kind and gentle. You have a good heart and you don't play games with my heart. I don't know how it happened but you've come to mean so much to me. I want to spend my days walking hand and hand with you under the whispering pines. I want to make love to you so that all the pines have to whisper about is our love. I do love you. I want you, I need you. I'm asking you to be my wife."

Tears sprung to her eyes as their gazes continued to hold. "I didn't know what to expect when I put these clothes on. I thought perhaps you'd be angry." She smiled. "Your words about our love being whispered among the pines are the loveliest I've ever heard. I'd love to be your wife, but I have a few questions."

He pulled her into his embrace. "Ask away."

She could feel his heart speed up and she was sure hers matched his. "Will I be expected to live in town after the wedding? Will you want children?"

He kissed the side of her neck and she shivered. "No and

yes. I think my goal is to have a town where we can both live. For now, we'll stay up on the mountain until we get that town built. We can decide then what we want to do but I want us to be together."

Standing on tiptoes, she wrapped her arms around his neck and brought his head down for a kiss. His firm lips softened a bit as they met hers. It was the sweetest moment she'd ever had. The feel of his hands running up and down her back as he opened his mouth to her made her moan. She pressed herself against him feeling his arousal.

"Ahem."

They sprung apart at the sound and looked toward the door. Old Barney stood right inside the door looking healthier than he'd ever looked.

He gave them a feeble smile. "I heard the news about you two getting hitched and all. I have to admit I scratched my head about you being a female, Miss Pat. I have somethin' I want you to have. Old Hans traded it to me a while back for some tobacco." He took a few steps forward. "Anyway here it is. I hope you like it."

Pat gasped when she saw what he held in his hand. It was her mother's brooch. Hans must have been the one to steal from her. She took the brooch and gave Barney a big hug. "This means the world to me. Thank you." He turned bright red when she kissed his cheek.

"The reverend said the wedding was private?"

Samuel stepped forward. "Yes, but the celebrating is for everyone."

Barney smiled and left.

"Here let me pin this on you. It sure is pretty. I like the green stone in the middle of the diamonds."

"They're glass, not diamonds." She waited while he pinned it on her.

"I know a thing or two about diamonds and these are real. The green stone is glass but the rest is real."

Her jaw dropped. "Da must have replaced the glass with diamonds. We did make a good strike before we came here. He should have told me."

"He probably meant to surprise you." He took her into his strong arms and held her.

"I know this sounds stupid but it's almost as though my father is giving his blessing to our marriage."

He rubbed his big hands up and down her back. "It's not stupid at all. It's sweet." He stepped back and smiled at her. "You're so lovely. Listen if you don't want to do this—"

"I do. I love you with all my heart. I think I have for a very long time. I want us to be married."

———

AFTER THE CEREMONY, Samuel tenderly kissed his bride. The way she kissed him back made his whole body tingle. He couldn't wait to undress her later and make sweet, passionate love to her. The kiss ended and he smiled. Her whole face glowed and her eyes were filled with happiness.

He'd placed guards outside the cookhouse to keep Linda away. All throughout the ceremony he waited for her, her father or his father to come marching through the door to stop the wedding. Now he could relax. Pat was his wife.

"Are you ready to greet the men?" he asked.

Pat nodded.

He took her hand and felt her tremble. "Some of them already saw you in your dress. I'm sure they all know by now. Plus they know a celebration means opening a keg. I don't think any of them will mind you're my wife."

The trust in her eyes humbled him. He never had anyone

believe in him the way she did. "Did I tell you how much I love you?"

Pat blushed. "If it's the same amount of love I have for you, then it is a great love."

He slanted his lips over hers and gave her a long lingering kiss. "Let's go celebrate."

EPILOGUE

 *wo Years Later*

PAT HUNG onto Samuel's hand as they waited for the ribbon cutting ceremony to mark the opening of the new school in the town of Pearce. It had taken many months of planning and a lot of work but they had built a town to be proud of. Best of all Samuel had treated her ideas as equal to his own.

Everyone waited for the new mayor Hank Blue to arrive. Samuel didn't want to be the mayor. He said he was busy enough with his lumber business and his soon to be growing family.

He reached down and put a protective hand on her ever increasing stomach. Gazing at him, she hoped that her love for him could be seen in her eyes. The smoldering gaze he returned gave her the answer.

"You know I wouldn't have minded living up on the mountain with you," she said.

"I know. It's not only because of the baby I want to live in town. I want you to myself. I couldn't believe all the *ailments* those rough timber men suddenly came up with just to be near you."

"No one was inappropriate."

"Just the same I'm glad to have you without interruption."

Pat blushed remembering a few of the interruptions they'd had. They'd whispered their love plenty of times up on the mountain. They'd gotten caught a few times too. Once by a bear. "I'll miss our afternoon naps."

"Naps is it?" Samuel laughed. "Yes, napping was my favorite part of the day."

She jabbed him playfully in the stomach. "Here comes Hank. It's time to be serious."

"Can we nap afterwards?"

Her face heated as she shook her head. Life was never boring with her lumberjack.

THE END

I'm so pleased you chose to read Whispered Love, and it's my sincere hope that you enjoyed the story. I would appreciate if you'd consider posting a review. This can help an author tremendously in obtaining a readership. My many thanks. ~ Kathleen

ABOUT THE AUTHOR

Sexy Cowboys and the Women Who Love Them...
Finalist in the 2012 and 2015 RONE Awards.
Top Pick, Five Star Series from the Romance Review.
Kathleen Ball writes contemporary and historical western
romance with great emotion and
memorable characters. Her books are award winners and
have appeared on best sellers lists including: Amazon's Best
Seller's List, All Romance Ebooks, Bookstrand, Desert
Breeze Publishing and Secret Cravings Publishing Best
Sellers list. She is the recipient of eight Editor's Choice
Awards, and The Readers' Choice Award for Ryelee's
Cowboy.
Winner of the Lear diamond award Best Historical Novel-
Cinders' Bride
There's something about a cowboy

f facebook.com/kathleenballwesternromance

🐦 twitter.com/kballauthor

📷 instagram.com/author_kathleenball

OTHER BOOKS BY KATHLEEN

Lasso Spring's Series
Callie's Heart

Lone Star Joy

Stetson's Storm

Dawson Ranch Series
Texas Haven

Ryelee's Cowboy

Cowboy Season Series
Summer's Desire

Autumn's Hope

Winter's Embrace

Spring's Delight

Mail Order Brides of Texas
Cinders' Bride

Keegan's Bride

Shane's Bride

Tramp's Bride

Poor Boy's Christmas

Oregon Trail Dreamin'

We've Only Just Begun

A Lifetime to Share

A Love Worth Searching For

So Many Roads to Choose

The Settlers

Greg

Juan

The Greatest Gift

Love So Deep

Luke's Fate

Whispered Love

Love Before Midnight

I'm Forever Yours

Finn's Fortune

24936175R00055